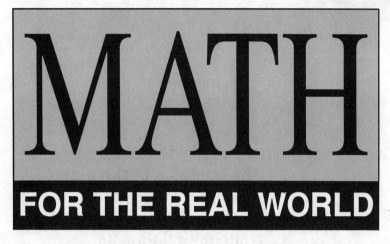

MATH
FOR THE REAL WORLD

BOOK TWO

Dolores Byrne Kimball

New Readers Press
Publishing Division of Laubach Literacy International
Syracuse, New York

This book is dedicated to
the students of the
Gavilan College/
San Benito County Education Center
Hollister, California

ISBN-08836-839-0

© 1990

New Readers Press
Publishing Division of Laubach Literacy International
Box 131, Syracuse, New York 13210

Printed in the United States of America

Editorial, design and production services: B&B Communications West, Inc.

9 8 7 6

Contents

UNIT 3

Measurement

UNIT 4

Adding and Subtracting Fractions

UNIT 5

Multiplying and Dividing Fractions

UNIT 6

Percents

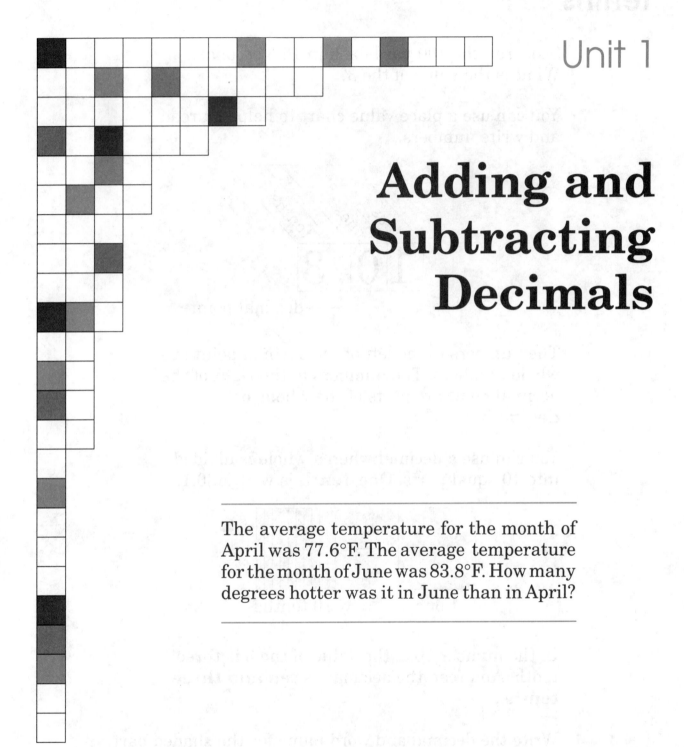

Adding and Subtracting Decimals

The average temperature for the month of April was 77.6°F. The average temperature for the month of June was 83.8°F. How many degrees hotter was it in June than in April?

CHAPTER 1

Tenths

Scott ran the 100-yard dash in 10.3 seconds. What is the value of the 3?

You can use a place value chart to help you read and write numbers.

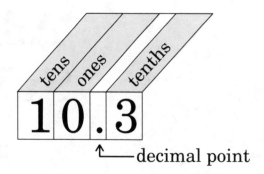

The numbers to the left of the decimal point are whole numbers. The numbers to the right of the decimal point are parts of the whole, or **decimals.**

You can use a decimal when a whole is divided into 10 equal parts. One **tenth** is written 0.1.

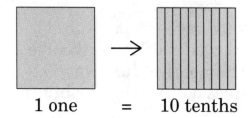

1 one   =   10 tenths

In the number 10.3, the value of the 3 is three tenths. You read the decimal as **ten and three tenths.**

Example: Write the decimal and word name for the shaded part.

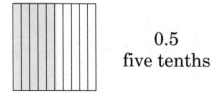

0.5
five tenths

Exercise 1-A

Write the decimal for the shaded part.

1.   _____

2.   _____

Exercise 1-B

Write the number in words.

3. 4.1 _____

4. 0.2 _____

5. 18.5 _____

6. 3.7 _____

Exercise 1-C

Write the decimal.

7. eight tenths _____

8. four tenths _____

9. six tenths _____

10. one tenth _____

11. 6 and 2 tenths _____

12. 9 and 6 tenths _____

13. 20 and 5 tenths _____

14. 32 and 1 tenth _____

15. fifty and three tenths _____

16. 23 and 6 tenths _____

17. sixteen and five tenths _____

18. 43 and 9 tenths _____

CHAPTER 2

Hundredths

Adrienne walked 2.45 miles on Tuesday. She uses a *pedometer* to measure the distance she walks every day. A pedometer measures the distance in **hundredths** of a mile.

You can use a decimal when a whole is divided into 100 equal parts. One **hundredth** is written 0.01.

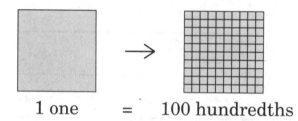

1 one   =   100 hundredths

The shaded part of the place value models below shows how far Adrienne walked.

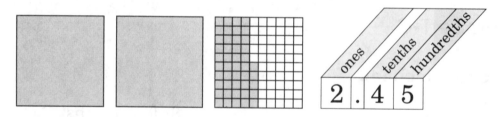

2 and 45 hundredths are shaded.

It is read as *two and forty-five hundredths.*

Example: How many hundredths are shaded? Write the decimal.

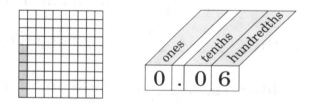

6 hundredths are shaded.
The decimal is written as 0.06.
It is read *six hundredths.*

Look at the place value chart. Why is there a zero in the tenths column?

Exercise 2-A

Write the decimal for the shaded part.

1. 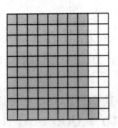 _____

2. _____   _____

Exercise 2-B

Write the number in words.

3. 0.07 _____

4. 1.34 _____

5. 7.19 _____

6. 15.86 _____

Exercise 2-C

Write the decimal.

7. 63 hundredths _____

8. two hundredths _____

9. 89 hundredths _____

10. four hundredths _____

11. 4 and 16 hundredths _____

12. 9 and 6 hundredths _____

13. 15 and 3 hundredths _____

14. 23 and 34 hundredths _____

15. 2 ones 3 tenths 2 hundredths _____

16. 6 ones 9 hundredths _____

17. 5 ones 1 tenth 2 hundredths _____

18. 6 tens 6 tenths _____

CHAPTER 3

Thousandths

Baseball players' batting averages are given to the nearest **thousandth.**

You can use a decimal when a whole is divided into 1,000 equal parts. One thousandth is written 0.001.

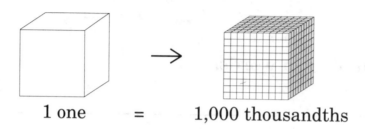

1 one   =   1,000 thousandths

Use the place value chart to help you read the numbers.

tens	ones	tenths	hundredths	thousandths
0.	3	4	8	
1.	6	2	4	
15.	0	0	7	

In the number 0.348, the 8 is in the thousandths place.
Its value is 8 thousandths.
It is read *three hundred forty-eight thousandths.*

In the number 1.624, the 4 is in the thousandths place.
Its value is 4 thousandths.
It is read *one and six hundred twenty-four thousandths.*

In the number 15.007, the 7 is in the thousandths place.
Its value is 7 thousandths.
It is read *fifteen and seven thousandths.*

Exercise 3-A

Write the number in words.

1. 0.003 _____

2. 1.107 _____

3. 12.349 _____

Exercise 3-B

Write the number.

4. 324 thousandths _____

5. 3 and 41 thousandths _____

6. 5 and 341 thousandths _____

7. 41 and 8 thousandths _____

Exercise 3-C

In the number 32.174 what digit is in the:

8. tens place? _____

9. hundredths place? _____

10. tenths place? _____

11. thousandths place? _____

 RITICAL THINKING

Use the cards at the right to solve.

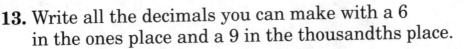

12. Write two decimals with a 1 in the thousandths place and a 3 in the tenths place.

_____

13. Write all the decimals you can make with a 6 in the ones place and a 9 in the thousandths place.

_____

CHAPTER 4

Comparing and Ordering Decimals

Comparing decimals is the same as comparing whole numbers. Start at the left and compare the digits.

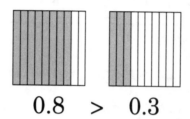 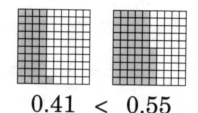

$$0.8 \ > \ 0.3 \qquad 0.41 \ < \ 0.55$$

Example: Compare 1.2 and 1.27.

To compare, write a zero after the 1.2. The value stays the same.

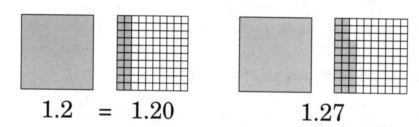

$$1.2 \ = \ 1.20 \qquad\qquad 1.27$$

Look at the shaded squares.

$$1.20 \ < 1.27$$
$$1.2 \ \ \ < 1.27$$

MENTAL MATH

You can compare numbers mentally.

$$1.62 \quad 1.79 \quad 1.99$$

$$1.62 < 1.79 < 1.99$$

These numbers are in order from least to greatest.

Exercise 4-A

Write <, >, or = to compare the decimals.

1. 0.2 _____ 0.8   **2.** 0.4 _____ 0.5   **3.** 0.6 _____ 6.0

4. 0.22 _____ 0.17   **5.** 0.30 _____ 0.10   **6.** 0.134 _____ 0.137

7. 4.11 _____ 4.13   **8.** 2.07 _____ 2.070   **9.** 3.12 _____ 3.012

10. 2.70 _____ 2.71   **11.** 3.169 _____ 3.147   **12.** 0.75 _____ 0.750

Exercise 4-B

Order from least to greatest.

13. 0.7, 0.2, 1.7 _____

14. 0.27, 0.35, 0.16 _____

15. 3.3, 3.33, 3.303 _____

16. 4.10, 4.01, 4.011, 4.101 _____

17. 0.34, 0.43, 0.52, 0.32 _____

MENTAL MATH

Use mental math. Write each number as a hundredths decimal.

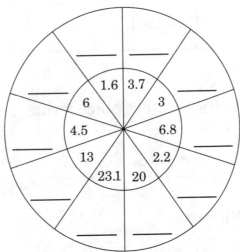

CHAPTER 5

Rounding Decimals

The quarterback of the football team averaged 7.64 yards per pass last season. You can round the decimal if you do not need to know the exact answer.

Rounding decimals is the same as rounding whole numbers. Look at the digit to the right of the place to be rounded.

Round down when the digit is 0, 1, 2, 3, or 4.
Round up when the digit is 5, 6, 7, 8, or 9.

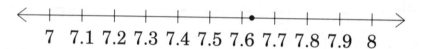

7   7.1 7.2 7.3 7.4 7.5 7.6 7.7 7.8 7.9   8

7.64 rounded to the nearest whole number is 8.
7.64 rounded to the nearest tenth is 7.6.

Example:

Number	Round to the nearest	Digit to the right	Is it 5 or more?	Round
46.59	whole number	5	yes	up to 47
13.71	tenth	1	no	down to 13.7
3.802	hundredth	2	no	down to 3.80

Example: Round 35.87 to its greatest place value.

35.87 ◁ — Look at the digit to the right of the tens place.

Round 35.87 up to 40.

Exercise 5-A

Round to the nearest whole number.

1. 3.2 _____

2. 6.7 _____

3. 3.85 _____

4. 6.75 _____

5. 33.21 _____

6. 27.52 _____

7. 39.07 _____

8. 42.51 _____

9. 82.17 _____

Exercise 5-B

Round to the nearest tenth.

10. 3.32 _____

11. 4.73 _____

12. 6.88 _____

13. 9.07 _____

14. 34.12 _____

15. 16.86 _____

16. 43.94 _____

17. 21.11 _____

18. 64.58 _____

Exercise 5-C

Round to the greatest place value.

19. 3.3 _____

20. 37.4 _____

21. 22.8 _____

22. 8.57 _____

23. 41.89 _____

24. 39.10 _____

25. 27.3 _____

26. 4.52 _____

27. 16.18 _____

Exercise 5-D

Round to the place of the underlined digit.

28. 1_6_.4 _____

29. 3._7_2 _____

30. 16._9_4 _____

31. 113._2_6 _____

32. 0._7_5 _____

33. 10_0_.12 _____

CHAPTER 6

Problem Solving Strategy: Estimating with Decimals

Megan is a salesperson for a tool company. She plans on leaving her office and making sales calls today. She visits Cy's Circular Saws and Dan's Security Doors in the morning. About how many miles will she travel?

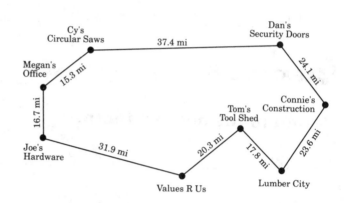

Sometimes you do not need an exact answer. You can estimate to solve a problem.

Use the map above to solve the problem. To estimate how many miles Megan traveled, round each number to the greatest place value.

$$
\begin{array}{rcl}
15.3 & \rightarrow & 20 \\
+\ 37.4 & \rightarrow & +\ 40 \\
\hline
& & 60
\end{array}
$$

Megan traveled about 60 miles.

Example: In the afternoon, Megan traveled from Dan's Security Doors to Connie's Construction and Lumber City. About how many miles did she travel in the afternoon?

To find out, use the map and estimate.

$$
\begin{array}{rcl}
24.1 & \rightarrow & 20 \\
+\ 23.6 & \rightarrow & +\ 20 \\
\hline
& & 40
\end{array}
$$

Round to the greatest place value.

Exercise 6-A

Estimate to solve.

1. Megan spent $8.93 on gasoline in the morning. She spent $4.23 on gasoline in the afternoon. About how much money did she spend on gasoline?

_____

2. Rob is making a fruit basket. He wants to buy 6 pounds of fruit. He gets 1.37 pounds of grapes, 2.73 pounds of apples, and 1.99 pounds of oranges. Does he have enough fruit?

_____

3. Jessica made $276.57 in commissions this week. Peter made $124.75. About how much more did Jessica make than Peter?

_____

4. Megan drove 100.4 miles the first day of her business trip. The second day, she drove 86.7 miles. About how many more miles did she drive the first day?

_____

5. Juan buys a novel for $27.23 and a bookmark for $2.19. About how much did he spend in all?

_____

6. Brian ordered cement at Connie's Construction. It was delivered in two shipments. The first shipment was 75.7 pounds. The second shipment was 175.8 pounds. About how many pounds of cement did Brian order?

_____

CHAPTER 7

Adding Decimals

Karen runs 1.35 miles on Monday and 4.19 miles on Tuesday. How many miles does she run in all?

To find out, add 1.35 and 4.19. When you add decimals, it is very important to keep the decimal points in line.

$$
\begin{array}{r}
1.35 \\
+\ 4.19 \\
\end{array}
\quad\rightarrow\quad
\begin{array}{r}
\overset{1}{} \\
1.35 \\
+\ 4.19 \\
\hline
5.54 \\
\end{array}
$$

Step 1 Line up the decimal points.

Step 2 Add the hundredths. Regroup if necessary.

Step 3 Add the tenths. Regroup if necessary.

Step 4 Add the ones.

Karen ran 5.54 miles.

Sometimes each decimal does not have the same number of places. When this happens, add a zero after the last digit of a decimal. Remember, writing a zero as a placeholder does not change its value.

Example: Add: 8.35 + 2.7

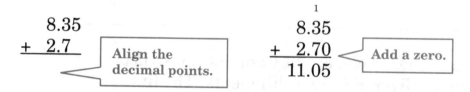

$$
\begin{array}{r}
8.35 \\
+\ 2.7 \\
\end{array}
\qquad\qquad
\begin{array}{r}
\overset{1}{} \\
8.35 \\
+\ 2.70 \\
\hline
11.05 \\
\end{array}
$$

Align the decimal points.   Add a zero.

CALCULATING

When you use a calculator to add decimals, you do not need to add the zero as a placeholder.

Add: 37.7 + 3.58

Press: 37.7 ⊞ 3.58 ⊟ 41.28

Exercise 7-A

Add.

1. 3.7 + 2.1	**2.** 4.9 + 2.6	**3.** 8.92 + 3.87	**4.** 6.39 + 4.87
5. 13.63 + 3.09	**6.** 16.35 + 4.89	**7.** 83.09 + 2.17	**8.** 19.08 + 42.71
9. 33.7 + 34.9	**10.** 13.84 + 1.76	**11.** 85.37 + 3.83	**12.** 3.87 + 50.38
13. 6.39 + 17.38	**14.** 43.89 + 12.63	**15.** 8.99 + 13.47	**16.** 15.99 + 13.17
17. 89.60 + 13.89	**18.** 52.89 + 18.80	**19.** 13.42 + 63.89	**20.** 33.89 + 14.63
21. 9.92 + 13.82	**22.** 16.39 + 14.81	**23.** 52.17 + 1.89	**24.** 33.17 + 23.89

Exercise 7-B

Add.

25.
$$\begin{array}{r} 16.5 \\ + 3 \\ \hline \end{array}$$

26.
$$\begin{array}{r} 8.92 \\ + 1.7 \\ \hline \end{array}$$

27.
$$\begin{array}{r} 3.7 \\ + 3.89 \\ \hline \end{array}$$

28.
$$\begin{array}{r} 32.7 \\ + 14.38 \\ \hline \end{array}$$

29.
$$\begin{array}{r} 0.72 \\ + 3.1 \\ \hline \end{array}$$

30.
$$\begin{array}{r} 8 \\ + 2.33 \\ \hline \end{array}$$

31.
$$\begin{array}{r} 14.1 \\ + 0.87 \\ \hline \end{array}$$

32.
$$\begin{array}{r} 33.9 \\ + 2.89 \\ \hline \end{array}$$

33.
$$\begin{array}{r} 14.63 \\ + 3.8 \\ \hline \end{array}$$

34.
$$\begin{array}{r} 9.75 \\ + 4.1 \\ \hline \end{array}$$

35.
$$\begin{array}{r} 93.16 \\ + 2.8 \\ \hline \end{array}$$

36.
$$\begin{array}{r} 5.9 \\ + 7.87 \\ \hline \end{array}$$

37.
$$\begin{array}{r} 44.89 \\ + 37.2 \\ \hline \end{array}$$

38.
$$\begin{array}{r} 16.7 \\ + 8.93 \\ \hline \end{array}$$

39.
$$\begin{array}{r} 13.63 \\ + 3.4 \\ \hline \end{array}$$

40.
$$\begin{array}{r} 58.7 \\ + 8.53 \\ \hline \end{array}$$

41.
$$\begin{array}{r} 22.7 \\ + 13.97 \\ \hline \end{array}$$

42.
$$\begin{array}{r} 6.72 \\ + 43.8 \\ \hline \end{array}$$

43.
$$\begin{array}{r} 13.98 \\ + 3.4 \\ \hline \end{array}$$

44.
$$\begin{array}{r} 2.8 \\ + 3.72 \\ \hline \end{array}$$

Exercise 7-C

Solve.

45. Mike has $10. He wants to buy a roll of film for
$3.79 and batteries for $5.20. Does he have
enough money?

_____

46. Rose rides her bicycle for 6.8 miles on Saturday
and 3.75 miles on Sunday. How many miles does
she ride in all?

_____

CHAPTER 8

Subtracting Decimals

The high temperature on Friday was 88.7°F. The high temperature on Saturday was 90.3°F. How much lower was the temperature on Friday?

To find out, subtract 88.7 from 90.3.

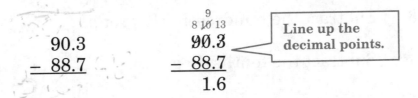

$$
\begin{array}{r} 90.3 \\ -\ 88.7 \end{array}
$$

$$
\begin{array}{r} \overset{\overset{9}{8\ \cancel{10}\ 13}}{\cancel{90}.\cancel{3}} \\ -\ 88.7 \\ \hline 1.6 \end{array}
$$

Line up the decimal points.

Step 1   Line up the decimal points.

Step 2   Subtract the tenths. Regroup.

Step 3   Subtract the ones. Regroup.

Step 4   Subtract the tens.

The temperature was 1.6°F lower on Friday.

Sometimes when you subtract decimals, each decimal does not have the same number of places. When this happens, add zeros as placeholders. Remember, adding a zero after the last digit of a decimal does not change its value.

Example: Subtract 4.75 from 9.2.

$$
\begin{array}{r} 9.2 \\ -\ 4.75 \end{array}
$$

$$
\begin{array}{r} \overset{8\ 11 10}{9.\cancel{2}0} \\ -\ 4.75 \\ \hline 4.45 \end{array}
$$

Add a zero.

Example: Subtract 6.39 from 42.

$$
\begin{array}{r} 42 \\ -\ 6.39 \\ \hline \end{array}
\qquad
\begin{array}{r} 42.00 \\ -\ 6.39 \\ \hline \end{array}
\qquad
\begin{array}{r} 42.00 \\ -\ 6.39 \\ \hline 35.61 \end{array}
$$

Step 1   Line up the decimal points.

Step 2   Add a zero in the tenths place and hundredths place.

Step 3   Subtract the hundredths. Regroup.

Step 4   Subtract the tenths. Regroup.

Step 5   Subtract the ones. Regroup.

Step 6   Subtract the tens.

Exercise 8-A

Subtract.

1. $\begin{array}{r} 0.8 \\ -\ 0.2 \\ \hline \end{array}$	**2.** $\begin{array}{r} 6.3 \\ -\ 4.1 \\ \hline \end{array}$	**3.** $\begin{array}{r} 5.8 \\ -\ 2.9 \\ \hline \end{array}$	**4.** $\begin{array}{r} 9.3 \\ -\ 4.2 \\ \hline \end{array}$
5. $\begin{array}{r} 16.7 \\ -\ 2.7 \\ \hline \end{array}$	**6.** $\begin{array}{r} 42.8 \\ -\ 3.4 \\ \hline \end{array}$	**7.** $\begin{array}{r} 36.8 \\ -\ 13.3 \\ \hline \end{array}$	**8.** $\begin{array}{r} 9.4 \\ -\ 2.2 \\ \hline \end{array}$
9. $\begin{array}{r} 33.1 \\ -\ 16.7 \\ \hline \end{array}$	**10.** $\begin{array}{r} 42.4 \\ -\ 6.8 \\ \hline \end{array}$	**11.** $\begin{array}{r} 52.5 \\ -\ 13.6 \\ \hline \end{array}$	**12.** $\begin{array}{r} 68.7 \\ -\ 13.9 \\ \hline \end{array}$
13. $\begin{array}{r} 4.38 \\ -\ 2.72 \\ \hline \end{array}$	**14.** $\begin{array}{r} 8.74 \\ -\ 3.89 \\ \hline \end{array}$	**15.** $\begin{array}{r} 37.84 \\ -\ 16.43 \\ \hline \end{array}$	**16.** $\begin{array}{r} 89.31 \\ -\ 43.87 \\ \hline \end{array}$

Exercise 8-B

Subtract.

17.	3.6 – 1	**18.**	8.39 – 3.2	**19.**	7.84 – 2.4	**20.**	13.53 – 7

21.	8 – 3.7	**22.**	7.8 – 3.92	**23.**	0.7 – 0.42	**24.**	0.9 – 0.36

25.	82.2 – 8.95	**26.**	16 – 4.81	**27.**	36.7 – 22.72	**28.**	43 – 8.73

29.	74.3 – 13.91	**30.**	62.6 – 43.74	**31.**	89.3 – 7.54	**32.**	52.9 – 1.79

Exercise 8-C

Solve.

33. Janice has a $5 bill. She spends $1.89 at the
card shop. How much change does she receive? _____

34. Daniel spends $89.50 on groceries and $29.43
on records. How much more does he spend on
groceries than on records? _____

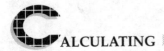 **C**ALCULATING

Use a calculator to find the differences.

35. 8 – 3.2 _____   **36.** 9 – 4.1 _____   **37.** $6 – $2.89 _____

APPLICATION

Batting Averages

Baseball players keep track of their batting performance with a **batting average**. A batting average is a record of the number of hits and the number of times at bat. This average is written as a decimal to the thousandths place.

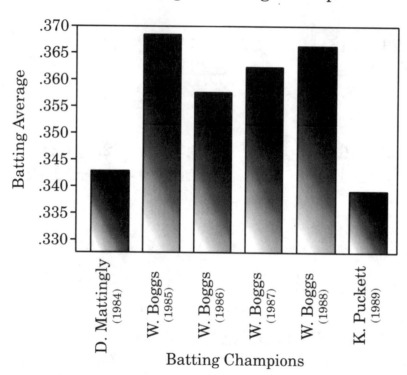

American League Batting Champions

Use the graph to answer the questions.

1. Who had a higher batting average, Kirby Puckett or Don Mattingly? _____

2. In which year did Wade Boggs have his highest batting average? _____

3. How much higher was Wade Boggs' batting average in 1988 than in 1987? _____

4. Which player had the highest batting average? _____

uiz for UNIT 1

Write the number in words.

1. 0.7 _____

2. 4.32 _____

3. 48.007 _____

Write the decimal.

4. 9 and 3 tenths _____   **5.** 4 and 9 hundredths _____

6. 3 and 8 thousandths _____   **7.** thirty-one thousandths _____

Compare.

8. 0.7 ___ 0.4   **9.** 4.17 ___ 4.017   **10.** 0.85 ___ 0.850

11. 4.123 ___ 4.321   **12.** 0.70 ___ 0.10   **13.** 13.824 ___ 13.249

Round to the greatest place value.

14. 4.5 _____   **15.** 63.9 _____   **16.** 2.8 _____

17. 16.7 _____   **18.** 43.84 _____   **19.** 16.17 _____

Add or subtract.

20.   6.3
        + 2.4

21.   8.9
        + 3.7

22.   4.1
        + 3.79

23.   3.9
        + 4.81

24.   6.9
        − 2.5

25.   8.7
        − 2.9

26.   32.1
        − 5.63

27.   42
        − 3.89

CUMULATIVE REVIEW

Circle the letter of the correct answer.

Write the number.

1. five tenths
   a. 5.0   c. 0.05
   b. 0.5   d. none of these

2. 7 and 6 thousandths
   a. 7.06   c. 7.006
   b. 7.6   d. none of these

3. nine and forty-three thousandths
   a. 9.043   c. 9.43
   b. 0.943   d. none of these

Compare the numbers.

4. 0.4 ___ 0.9
   a. >   c. =
   b. <   d. none of these

5. 3.15 ___ 3.150
   a. >   c. =
   b. <   d. none of these

6. 7.895 ___ 7.947
   a. >   c. =
   b. <   d. none of these

Round to the greatest place value.

7. 3.7
   a. 3.8   c. 4
   b. 3   d. none of these

8. 4.88
   a. 5   c. 4
   b. 4.9   d. none of these

Add.

9. 1.24 + 3.87
   a. 1.627   c. 4.93
   b. 5.11   d. none of these

10. 33.87 + 41.98
    a. 74.75   c. 75.85
    b. 38.068   d. none of these

11. 4.7 + 3.92
    a. 8.62   c. 7.99
    b. 33.9   d. none of these

Subtract.

12. 8.7 - 3.8
    a. 5.9   c. 8.32
    b. 4.9   d. none of these

13. 12 - 6.7
    a. 6.3   c. 5.3
    b. 5.93   d. none of these

14. 18.38 - 4.6
    a. 13.49   c. 17.3
    b. 12.79   d. none of these

Multiplying and Dividing Decimals

The length of Tim's living room is 18.6 feet and the width is 12.4 feet. What is the area of the room?

CHAPTER 9

Multiplying Decimals by Whole Numbers

When you multiply a decimal by a whole number, the product will have the same number of decimal places as the decimal.

Example: Multiply 2.34 x 2.

You can use place value models to show 2.34.

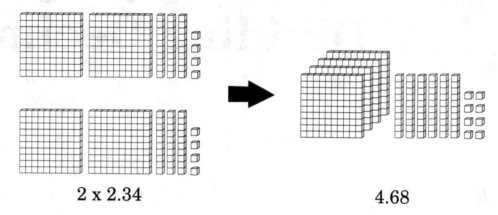

2 x 2.34   4.68

Multiply decimals as you do whole numbers.

$$\begin{array}{r} 2.34 \\ \times \underline{2} \end{array} \qquad \begin{array}{r} 2.34 \\ \times \underline{2} \\ 4.68 \end{array}$$ ⟵ two decimal places

⟵ two decimal places

Step 1   Multiply 4 hundredths by 2.

Step 2   Multiply 3 tenths by 2.

Step 3   Multiply 2 ones by 2.

2.34 x 2 = 4.68

Multiplication can be thought of as repeated addition.

$$\begin{array}{r} 2.34 \\ \times \underline{2} \\ 4.68 \end{array} \qquad \begin{array}{r} 2.34 \\ + \underline{2.34} \\ 4.68 \end{array}$$

Sometimes when you multiply decimals by a
whole number, you need to regroup.

Example: Multiply 32.85 x 7.

Step 1	Step 2	Step 3
32.85	32.85	32.85 $\longleftarrow$ 2 decimal places
x 7	x 7	x 7
22995	22995	229.95 $\longleftarrow$ 2 decimal places

Step 1   Multiply as you would with whole numbers.

Step 2   Count the decimal places.

Step 3   Write the decimal point in the product.

Example: The Sock Hop was having a clearance sale.
Maggie bought 32 pairs of socks for $1.89 each.
How much did she spend at the sale?

To find out, multiply.

```
  $1.89              $1.89  ←—— 2 decimal places
x    32            x    32
   378                378
   567                567
  6048              $60.48  ←—— 2 decimal places
```

Example: Multiply 38.427 by 3.

```
   38.427
   38.427            38.427  ←—— 3 decimal places
 + 38.427          x      3
  115.281           115.281  ←—— 3 decimal places
```

Exercise 9-A

Multiply.

1. 0.36
    x 4

2. 0.74
    x 9

3. 0.82
    x 6

4. 3.8
    x 5

5. 734.2
    x 3

6. 89.43
    x 7

7. 12.8
    x 24

8. 73.89
    x 17

9. 89.7
    x 42

10. $41.44
    x 89

11. 9.189
    x 407

12. 8.274
    x 209

13. 22.94
    x 821

14. $62.17
    x 75

15. 6.127
    x 387

16. 9.194
    x 217

17. 5.812
    x 319

18. 43.82
    x 15

19. $16.89
    x 425

20. 62.3
    x 143

Exercise 9-B

Solve.

21. The scout troop sold 457 boxes of cookies. Each box sells for $2.25. How much money did they make from the cookie sale? _____

22. Marisa bought her grandson 3 books. The price of each book was $10.95. How much did she spend in all? _____

CHAPTER 10

Multiplying Decimals

You can use decimal models to show what happens when you multiply decimals. This model shows 0.4 x 0.2.

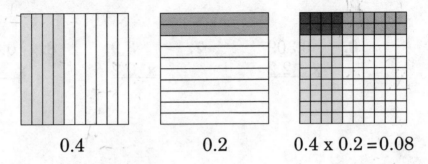

0.4   0.2   0.4 x 0.2 = 0.08

When you multiply tenths by tenths, the product is in hundredths.

Look at the hundredths model above. The shaded area that overlaps four tenths and two tenths is the product, or 8 hundredths.

When you multiply hundredths by tenths, the product is in thousandths.

Example: Multiply 3.82 x 2.7.

$$\begin{array}{r} 3.82 \\ \times\quad 2.7 \\ \hline 10.314 \end{array}$$

In general, if you add the number of decimal places in each factor, you will get the number of decimal places in the product.

$$\begin{array}{r} 3.82 \\ \times\quad 4 \\ \hline 15.28 \end{array}$$ ⟵ 2 decimal places
⟵ 0 decimal places
⟵ 2 decimal places

$$\begin{array}{r} 61.8 \\ \times\quad 0.67 \\ \hline 41.406 \end{array}$$ ⟵ 1 decimal place
⟵ 2 decimal places
⟵ 3 decimal places

Multiply.

1. 0.7
    x 0.8

2. 0.5
    x 0.9

3. 0.36
    x 0.7

4. 0.83
    x 0.5

5. 12.7
    x 0.9

6. 0.309
    x 2.2

7. 3.9
    x 0.2

8. 0.412
    x 2.7

9. 13.413
    x 3.7

10. 27.2
     x 8.9

11. 14.189
     x 6.7

12. 0.7
     x 148.3

13. 2.62
     x 142.8

14. 2.714
     x 23.9

15. 12.7
     x 3.6

16. 4.176
     x 0.32

17. 31.19
     x 0.72

18. 13.8
     x 147.9

19. 18.73
     x 20.1

20. 0.9
     x 42.8

Exercise 10-B

Use a calculator and multiply.

CALCULATING

21. 33.7 x 41.9 x 3.7 _____

22. 1.7 x 82.3 x 4.175 _____

CHAPTER 11

Dividing Decimals by Whole Numbers

Dividing decimals by whole numbers is the same as dividing whole numbers. However, you must remember to write a decimal point in the quotient.

Example: Divide: $9\overline{)13.5}$

Step 1	Step 2
$\begin{array}{r} 1\,5 \\ 9\overline{)13.5} \\ -\,9 \\ \hline 4\,5 \\ -4\,5 \\ \hline 0 \end{array}$	$\begin{array}{r} 1.5 \\ 9\overline{)13.5} \\ -\,9 \\ \hline 4\,5 \\ -4\,5 \\ \hline 0 \end{array}$

Step 1   Divide as you would with whole numbers.

Step 2   Write the decimal point in the quotient above the decimal point in the dividend.

When dividing decimals, you may need to add a zero in the quotient.

Example: Divide: $6\overline{)0.084}$

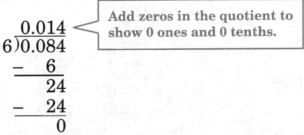

$$\begin{array}{r} 0.014 \\ 6\overline{)0.084} \\ -\quad 6 \\ \hline 24 \\ -\quad 24 \\ \hline 0 \end{array}$$

> Add zeros in the quotient to show 0 ones and 0 tenths.

When dividing decimals, you may need to add a zero in the dividend. Remember, when you add a zero after the last digit of a decimal, the value stays the same.

Example: Divide: $18\overline{)2.43}$

Step 1

$$
\begin{array}{r}
135 \\
18\overline{)2.430} \\
-18 \\
\hline
63 \\
-54 \\
\hline
90 \\
-90 \\
\hline
0
\end{array}
$$

Step 2

$$
\begin{array}{r}
0.135 \\
18\overline{)2.430} \\
-18 \\
\hline
63 \\
-54 \\
\hline
90 \\
-90 \\
\hline
0
\end{array}
$$

Step 1 Divide as you would with whole numbers. Add a zero to the dividend to complete the division.

Step 2 Write the decimal point in the quotient above the decimal point in the dividend.

Example: Marcella is knitting a baby blanket. She needs 189.8 grams of yarn. Each package of yarn is 52 grams. How many packages of yarn does she need?

To find out, divide.

$$
\begin{array}{r}
3.65 \\
52\overline{)189.80} \\
-156 \\
\hline
33\ 8 \\
-\ 31\ 2 \\
\hline
2\ 60 \\
-\ 2\ 60 \\
\hline
0
\end{array}
$$

Marcella needs to buy *four* packages of yarn. The quotient, 3.65, must be rounded up to the nearest whole number so that Marcella will have enough yarn to finish the blanket.

Exercise 11-A

Divide.

1. $3\overline{)34.5}$ **2.** $6\overline{)10.5}$ **3.** $7\overline{)9.8}$ **4.** $5\overline{)107.5}$

5. $8\overline{)83.2}$ **6.** $4\overline{)29.68}$ **7.** $9\overline{)594.9}$ **8.** $6\overline{)0.108}$

9. $3\overline{)9.321}$ **10.** $8\overline{)0.56}$ **11.** $32\overline{)2.4256}$ **12.** $39\overline{)10.062}$

13. $15\overline{)15.6}$ **14.** $27\overline{)64.8}$ **15.** $41\overline{)224.27}$ **16.** $69\overline{)1.4076}$

17. $52\overline{)2.8444}$ **18.** $62\overline{)1.736}$ **19.** $21\overline{)770.7}$ **20.** $17\overline{)5.2479}$

CHAPTER 12

Multiplying or Dividing by Powers of 10

You can multiply by a power of 10 mentally.

Multiply by 10	Multiply by 100	Multiply by 1,000
10 x 2.43 = 24.3	100 x 6.214 = 621.4	1000 x 3.8724 = 3,872.4
10 x 24.3 = 243	100 x 62.14 = 6,214	1000 x 38.724 = 38,724
10 x 243 = 2,430	100 x 621.4 = 62,140	1000 x 387.24 = 387,240

MENTAL MATH

Multiplying by 10 moves the decimal point one place to the right. Multiplying by 100 moves the decimal point two places to the right. Multiplying by 1,000 moves the decimal point three places to the right.

Multiplying by a power of 10 makes a greater number.

You can divide by a power of 10 mentally.

Divide by 10	Divide by 100	Divide by 1,000
32.5 ÷ 10 = 3.25	284.3 ÷ 100 = 2.843	4,783.5 ÷ 1,000 = 4.7835
3.25 ÷ 10 = 0.325	28.43 ÷ 100 = 0.2843	478.35 ÷ 1,000 = 0.47835
0.325 ÷ 10 = 0.0325	2.843 ÷ 100 = 0.02843	47.835 ÷ 1,000 = 0.047835

MENTAL MATH

Dividing by 10 moves the decimal point one place to the left. Dividing by 100 moves the decimal point two places to the left. Dividing by 1,000 moves the decimal point three places to the left.

Dividing by a power of 10 makes a lesser number.

Exercise 12-A

Multiply mentally.

1. 10 x 3.97 _____

2. 10 x 0.09 _____

3. 10 x 3.7 _____

4. 100 x 8.87 _____

5. 100 x 4.63 _____

6. 100 x 0.853 _____

7. 1,000 x 2.43 _____

8. 1,000 x 38.16 _____

9. 1,000 x 0.09 _____

Exercise 12-B

Divide mentally.

10. 8.7 ÷ 10 _____

11. 12.83 ÷ 10 _____

12. 0.04 ÷ 10 _____

13. 5.9 ÷ 100 _____

14. 0.82 ÷ 100 _____

15. 0.893 ÷ 100 _____

16. 7.143 ÷ 1,000 _____

17. 4.16 ÷ 1,000 _____

18. 39.12 ÷ 1,000 _____

Exercise 12-C

Multiply or divide mentally.

19. 100 x 3.47 _____

20. 10 x 0.763 _____

21. 834.6 ÷ 1,000 _____

22. 0.16 ÷ 10 _____

23. 1,000 x 85.1 _____

24. 9.198 ÷ 100 _____

25. 0.659 ÷ 10 _____

26. 12.07 ÷ 10 _____

CHAPTER 13

Problem Solving Strategy: Organizing Information in a Table

Barbara wants to go to the beauty salon to get a haircut, a permanent, and a manicure. She reads these ads in the newspaper to decide which salon has the least expensive rates.

Shirley's Shears	
Haircut	$20.25
Manicure	$15.99
Tints	$38.76
Permanent	$59.88

Chuck's Cutting Crib	
Haircut	$10.00
Manicure	$29.95
Tints	$18.70
Permanent	$50.00

Carole's Comb Out	
Haircut	$35.85
Manicure	$21.89
Tints	$70.89
Permanent	$61.45

She decides to make a table to organize the information.

Prices at each Salon

Salon	Haircut	Permanent	Manicure	Total
Shirley's	$20.25	$59.88	$15.99	$96.12
Chuck's	$10.00	$50.00	$29.95	$89.95
Carole's	$35.85	$61.45	$21.89	$119.19

Barbara's table is organized in such a way that it is easy to add the prices. She has columns that are labeled and rows that give the prices for each service. Barbara can see from the Total column that it would cost less to have a haircut, permanent, and manicure at Chuck's Cutting Crib.

Carole's Comb Out salon sells shampoo, conditioner, gel, and mousse. Use Carole's receipts to complete the table.

Sales at **Carole's Comb Out**

Day	Shampoo	Conditioner	Gel	Mousse	Total
Monday	3	0	6	0	9
1. Tuesday					
2. Wednesday					
3. Thursday					
4. Friday					

Monday
Shampoo
3 bottles
6 gels

Tuesday
18 Conditioner
3 mousse

Wednesday
13 Shampoo
19 Mousse

Thursday
12 Conditioner
16 gel

Friday
14 Shampoo
10 Conditioner

Use the table to answer the questions.

5. On which day were the most products sold?

_____

6. Was more shampoo or conditioner sold this week? _____

7. How many jars of gel were sold altogether this week? _____

8. On which day of the week were the most bottles of shampoo sold? _____

9. How many products did Carole sell altogether this week? _____

CHAPTER 14

Dividing by Tenths

Look at the place value models. Each strip represents 1 tenth, or 0.1.

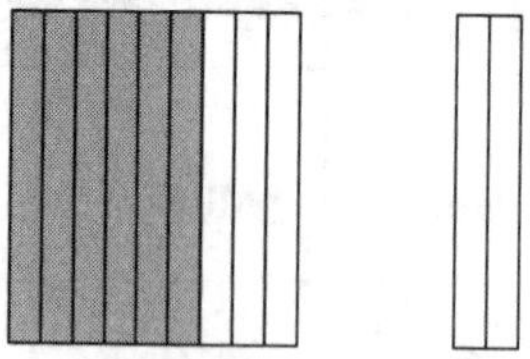

How many times can you match the two tenths strip with the shaded part of the tenths model?

This model shows 0.6 ÷ 0.2 = 0.3. To make dividing easier, you can also make the divisor a whole number by multiplying the divisor and the dividend by the same power of 10.

Example: Divide 6.8 by 0.4.

Step 1   [10 x 0.4] → $0.4\overline{)6.8}$ ← [10 x 6.8]

Step 2 $0.4\overline{)6.8}$

Step 3 $\begin{array}{r} 17 \\ 4\overline{)68} \end{array}$

Step 1 Multiply the divisor and the dividend by a power of 10.

Step 2 Move the decimal points one place to the right.

Step 3 Divide.

Check by multiplying.

17 x 0.4 = 6.8

Divide 4.23 by 0.9.

Step 1   Multiply the divisor and the dividend by 10.

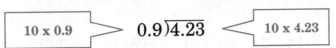

Step 2   Move the decimal points to the right.

$$0.9\overline{)42.3}$$

Step 3   Divide.

$$\begin{array}{r} 4.7 \\ 9\overline{)42.3} \\ -36 \\ \hline 6\,3 \\ -6\,3 \\ \hline 0 \end{array}$$

Exercise 14-A

Divide.

1. $0.6\overline{)7.2}$ 2. $0.4\overline{)2.2}$ 3. $0.7\overline{)4.41}$ 4. $0.3\overline{)0.267}$

5. $0.8\overline{)50.08}$ 6. $0.5\overline{)0.32}$ 7. $0.2\overline{)6.22}$ 8. $0.9\overline{)11.07}$

9. $1.3\overline{)85.02}$ 10. $6.2\overline{)2.232}$ 11. $4.9\overline{)15.729}$ 12. $7.2\overline{)30.6}$

Exercise 14-B

Divide.

13. $3.2\overline{)5.28}$ **14.** $4.9\overline{)22.393}$ **15.** $6.2\overline{)2.9636}$ **16.** $8.9\overline{)2.136}$

17. $4.1\overline{)1.5129}$ **18.** $2.2\overline{)2.1186}$ **19.** $5.8\overline{)182.12}$ **20.** $3.7\overline{)3.145}$

21. $31.2\overline{)196.56}$ **22.** $49.7\overline{)62.125}$ **23.** $50.6\overline{)23.782}$ **24.** $13.8\overline{)3.726}$

Exercise 14-C

Solve.

25. James drove 111.54 miles on a business trip. He averaged 50.7 miles per hour. How many hours did James drive?   _____

CALCULATING

You can use the constant feature on a calculator to find the quotient to division exercises without using the ÷ key.

Example: 36.6 ÷ 6.1. Press:

The number of times you pressed ⊟ to get 0 is the quotient, 6.

Find the quotient without using the ⊡ key.

26. 2.1 ÷ 0.7 _____   **27.** 1.6 ÷ 0.2 _____   **28.** 16.4 ÷ 4.1 _____

Dividing by Hundredths and Thousandths

A chemist has 29.04 grams of a substance needed to perform an experiment. She must put 0.24 grams into each test tube. How many test tubes does she need?

To find out, divide 29.04 by 0.24. Remember, when the divisor is a decimal, multiply it by a power of 10 to make a whole number.

Step 1   Multiply the divisor and the dividend by 100.

$$\boxed{100 \times 0.24} \quad 0.24\overline{)29.04} \quad \boxed{100 \times 29.04}$$

Step 2   Move the decimal points two places to the right.

$$0.24\overline{)29.04}$$

Step 3   Divide. $24\overline{)2904}$ with quotient 121

The chemist will need 121 test tubes.

Example: Divide 2.25 by 0.9.

$$\boxed{100 \times 0.09} \quad 0.09\overline{)2.25} \quad \boxed{100 \times 2.25}$$

$$0.09\overline{)2.25}$$

$$9\overline{)225} \text{ with quotient } 25$$

To divide a decimal by thousandths, multiply the divisor and dividend by 1,000. Sometimes you may need to add a zero in the dividend to complete the division.

Example: Divide 797.44 by 0.623.

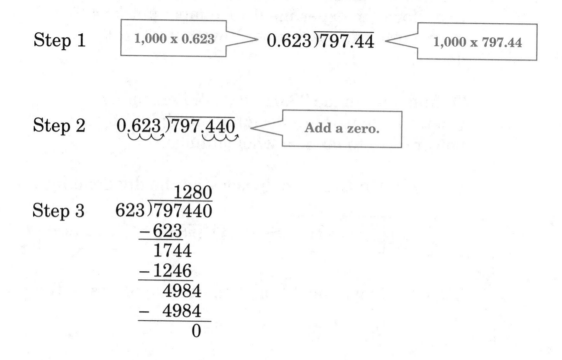

Step 1   1,000 x 0.623 ——> $0.623\overline{)797.44}$ <—— 1,000 x 797.44

Step 2 $0.623\overline{)797.440}$ <—— Add a zero.

Step 3
$$
\begin{array}{r}
1280 \\
623\overline{)797440} \\
-\underline{623} \\
1744 \\
-\underline{1246} \\
4984 \\
-\underline{4984} \\
0
\end{array}
$$

Example: Divide 8.2755 by 3.065.

$$3.065\overline{)8.2755}$$

Step 1   1,000 x 3.065 ——> $3.065\overline{)8.2755}$ <—— 1,000 x 8.2755

Step 2 $3.065\overline{)8.2755}$

Step 3
$$
\begin{array}{r}
2.7 \\
3.065\overline{)8275.5} \\
-\underline{6130} \\
2145\ 5 \\
-\underline{2145\ 5} \\
0
\end{array}
$$

Exercise 15-A

Divide.

1. $0.08\overline{)2.104}$ **2.** $0.04\overline{)15.6}$ **3.** $0.06\overline{)1.35}$ **4.** $0.09\overline{)5.742}$

5. $0.11\overline{)4.983}$ **6.** $0.05\overline{)11.5}$ **7.** $0.03\overline{)1.569}$ **8.** $0.02\overline{)1.928}$

9. $0.17\overline{)9.40525}$ **10.** $0.014\overline{)11.9588}$ **11.** $8.26\overline{)51.4598}$

12. $0.247\overline{)15.5363}$ **13.** $0.743\overline{)2.57821}$ **14.** $0.812\overline{)1.37228}$

Exercise 15-B

Avocados sell for $1.09 each. Tell how many were purchased for each sale.

15. $6.54 _____   **16.** $3.27 _____   **17.** $16.35 _____

APPLICATION

Area

Suppose you want to carpet the family room. You can find the *area* of a room by multiplying the length times the width.

The length is 20 feet.

The width is 14 feet.

Multiply 20 x 14 to find the area.

Area = 20 x 14

Area = 280

The area of the family room is 280 square feet.

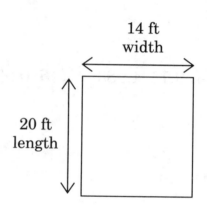

What is the area? Complete.

1. 0.56 / 0.36

_____ square units

2. 0.7 / 0.6

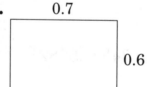

_____ square units

3. 9.37 / 3

_____ square units

4. 0.93 / 0.93

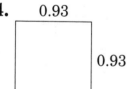

_____ square units

5. 0.85 / 0.17

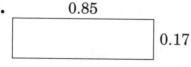

_____ square units

6. 3.89 / 7

_____ square units

Quiz for **UNIT 2**

Multiply.

1.   0.24
     x   6

2.   0.92
     x   8

3.   4.6
     x   3

4.   24.7
     x   18

5. $19.25
     x   324

6.   0.809
     x   0.7

7.   0.82
     x   0.5

8.   0.319
     x   3.7

9.   18.43
     x   16.1

10.   13.7
     x   8.4

11.   6.3
     x   124.73

12.   0.8
     x   113.9

Divide.

13. $5 \overline{)22.6}$

14. $9 \overline{)4.05}$

15. $14 \overline{)3466.4}$

16. $58 \overline{)31.726}$

17. $10 \overline{)4.683}$

18. $0.7 \overline{)43.75}$

19. $0.8 \overline{)17.2}$

20. $0.3 \overline{)16.92}$

21. $0.14 \overline{)8.876}$

22. $0.73 \overline{)32.2733}$

23. $0.256 \overline{)0.8192}$

CUMULATIVE REVIEW

Circle the letter of the correct answer.

Write the number.

1. sixteen and six hundredths

    a. 16.6   c. 16.06
    b. 16.006   d. none of these

2. nine and forty-five thousandths

    a. 9.0045   c. 9.045
    b. 9.45   d. none of these

Add.

3. 8.23 + 2.46

    a. 10.69   c. 0.169
    b. 1.69   d. none of these

4. 32.17 + 9.87

    a. 42.4   c. 41.04
    b. 42.04   d. none of these

Subtract.

5. 32 - 4.32

    a. 276.8   c. 27.68
    b. 2.768   d. none of these

6. 34.7 - 12.4

    a. 2.13   c. 2.23
    b. 22.3   d. none of these

7. 9.49 - 4.1

    a. 53.9   c. 0.539
    b. 5.39   d. none of these

Multiply.

8. 0.703 x 0.9

    a. 6.327   c. 63.27
    b. 0.6327   d. none of these

9. 0.7 x 112.7

    a. 78.89   c. 7.889
    b. 788.9   d. none of these

10. $18.23 x 412

    a. $7,510.76   c. $75,107.60
    b. $751.76   d. none of these

Divide.

11. 249.2 ÷ 4

    a. 6.23   c. 0.623
    b. 62.3   d. none of these

12. 3.924 ÷ 10

    a. 392.4   c. 0.3924
    b. 39.24   d. none of these

13. 294.435 ÷ 0.45

    a. 65.43   c. 6.543
    b. 654.3   d. none of these

Solve.

14. Marty traveled 68.5 miles on his bicycle last week. He rode 13.7 miles per hour. How many hours did he ride?

    a. 68.5   c. 4
    b. 5   d. none of these

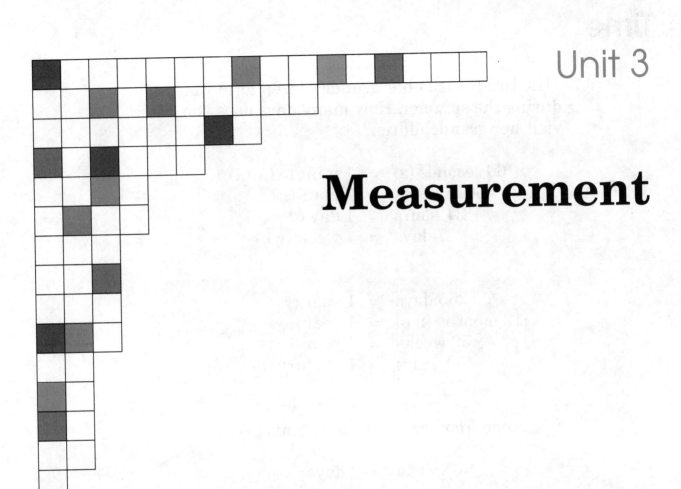

Measurement

Alex lives in Chicago. He made a long distance phone call to his father in Seattle at 8:50 P.M. CST. What time was it in Seattle?

CHAPTER 16

Time

Mrs. Brady visits her grandchildren for 6 weeks during the summer. How many days does she visit her grandchildren?

60 seconds (s)	=	1 minute (min)
60 minutes	=	1 hour (h)
24 hours	=	1 day (d)
7 days	=	1 week (wk)

365 days	=	1 year (y)
12 months (mo)	=	1 year
52 weeks	=	1 year
100 years	=	1 century (c)

To change from weeks to days, multiply.

6 weeks	=	? days
1 week	=	7 days
6 x 7	=	42
6 weeks	=	42 days

Mrs. Brady's visit lasted for 42 days.

Example: How many hours is 150 minutes?

To change units of time to a larger unit, divide.

150 minutes	=	? hours
60 minutes	=	1 hour
150 ÷ 60	=	2.5
150 minutes	=	2.5 hours

2 hours
30 minutes

Exercise 16-A

Complete.

1. 2 h = _____ min   **2.** 2 d = _____ h   **3.** 4 min = _____ s

4. 12 h = _____ min   **5.** 300 s = _____ min   **6.** 1 h = _____ s

7. 6 min = _____ s   **8.** 1 d = _____ min   **9.** 210 min = _____ h

10. 1 d = _____ s   **11.** _____ min = 900 s   **12.** _____ wk = 168 h

13. _____ h = 2 d   **14.** 280 d = _____ wk   **15.** _____ min = 720 s

16. 5 d = _____ h   **17.** _____ y = 730 d   **18.** 10 y = _____ mo

19. _____ mo = 2.5 y   **20.** 35 d = _____ wk   **21.** 360 min = _____ h

22. _____ wk = 5 y   **23.** _____ y = 2 c   **24.** 96 mo = _____ y

25. 4 c = _____ y   **26.** 84 d = _____ wk   **27.** 4 y = _____ mo

Exercise 16-B

Solve.

28. Walter spends 3 weeks in Mexico. How many days is that?

29. Diana taped a movie that was 1 hour 55 minutes. How many minutes was the movie?

30. The airline flight lasted 3 hours. How many seconds was the flight?

31. Mary called her daughter-in-law on Saturday. The call lasted 39 minutes. How many seconds did the call last?

_____

CHAPTER 17

Adding and Subtracting Time

Janice works part-time as a cashier. She worked
5 h 15 min on Monday and 3 h 55 min on
Wednesday. What is the total time she worked?

To find out, add.

Step 1   Add the minutes. Regroup.

$$\overset{1}{5} \text{ h} \quad 15 \text{ min}$$
$$+ \; 3 \text{ h} \quad \underline{55 \text{ min}}$$
$$\cancel{70 \text{ min}}$$
$$10 \text{ min}$$

> 60 min = 1 h so
> 70 min = 1 h 10 min

Step 2   Add the hours.

$$\overset{1}{5} \text{ h} \quad 15 \text{ min}$$
$$+ \; \underline{3 \text{ h} \quad 55 \text{ min}}$$
$$9 \text{ h} \quad 10 \text{ min}$$

Janice worked 9 h 10 min.

Example: It took Tim 17 minutes 14 seconds to complete a
typing test. It took Maddie 14 minutes 39 seconds
to complete the same test. How much longer did
it take Tim to finish the test?

To find out, subtract.

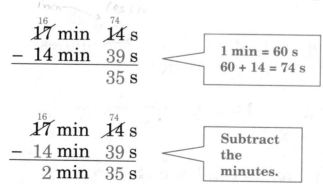

$$\overset{16}{\cancel{17}} \text{ min} \quad \overset{74}{\cancel{14}} \text{ s}$$
$$- \; 14 \text{ min} \quad \underline{39 \text{ s}}$$
$$35 \text{ s}$$

> 1 min = 60 s
> 60 + 14 = 74 s

$$\overset{16}{\cancel{17}} \text{ min} \quad \overset{74}{\cancel{14}} \text{ s}$$
$$- \; \underline{14 \text{ min} \quad 39 \text{ s}}$$
$$2 \text{ min} \quad 35 \text{ s}$$

> Subtract
> the
> minutes.

It took Tim 2 min 35 s longer to complete the
test.

Exercise 17-A

Add.

1.   2 hours   4 minutes
       + 3 hours   15 minutes

2.   16 minutes   32 seconds
       + 4 minutes   38 seconds

3.   19 hours   55 minutes
       + 2 hours   17 minutes

4.   23 minutes   14 seconds
      + 10 minutes   52 seconds

Exercise 17-B

Subtract.

5.   6 hours   35 minutes
       − 2 hours   10 minutes

6.   10 minutes   5 seconds
       − 3 minutes   46 seconds

7.   32 minutes   10 seconds
      − 10 minutes   39 seconds

8.   11 hours   14 minutes
       − 8 hours   22 minutes

Exercise 17-C

Solve.

9. Raymond cooks his special chili for 2 hours 45 minutes. Max cooks his chili 30 minutes longer than Raymond cooks his. How long does Max cook his chili?

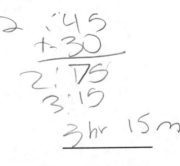

10. The drive from Kelley's house to her daughter's house took 3 hours 10 minutes during rush hour traffic. It normally takes 2 hours 15 minutes. How much longer does the drive take during rush hour?

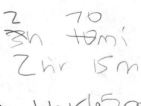

CHAPTER 18

Elapsed Time

Emily arrived at the meeting at 9:45 A.M. The meeting lasted until 12:15 P.M. How long did the meeting last?

To find out, subtract.

$$\begin{array}{ccc}
12{:}15 \text{ P.M.} & \rightarrow & \overset{11}{\cancel{12}} \text{ hours } \overset{75}{\cancel{15}} \text{ minutes} \\
9{:}45 \text{ A.M.} & \rightarrow & \underline{-\ 9 \text{ hours } 45 \text{ minutes}} \\
& & 2 \text{ hours } 30 \text{ minutes}
\end{array}$$

The meeting lasted for 2 hours 30 minutes.

Example: Wayne left for the airport at 6:30 P.M. It took 1 hour 10 minutes to get to the airport by car. What time did Wayne get to the airport?

MENTAL MATH

You can solve this problem mentally.

Think: 6:30 P.M. to 7:30 P.M. is 1 hour.
         7:30 P.M. and 10 minutes is 7:40 P.M.

Wayne arrived at the airport at 7:40 P.M.

Example: It takes Martin 2 hours 30 minutes to cook and eat dinner. He starts at 5:30 P.M. Then he rides his bicycle for 1 hour 15 minutes before he gets ready for bed. What times does Martin get ready for bed?

$$\begin{array}{ccc}
5{:}30 \text{ P.M.} \rightarrow & 5 \text{ hours } 30 \text{ minutes} & \\
& \underline{+\ 2 \text{ hours } 30 \text{ minutes}} & \\
& 8 \text{ hours } \ 0 \text{ minutes} & \leftarrow 8{:}00 \text{ P.M.}
\end{array}$$

Think: 8:00 P.M. to 9:00 P.M. is 1 hour.
         9:00 P.M. and 15 minutes is 9:15 P.M.

Martin gets ready for bed at 9:15 P.M.

Exercise 18-A

Solve.

1. Brian starts work at 8:45 A.M. He wakes up at 6:30 A.M. How much time does Brian have to get dressed and get to work? _____

2. Rose wants to watch a late night talk show on TV. It starts at 12:35 A.M. and ends at 1:15 A.M. How long is the show? _____

3. Krista gets home from work at 7:30 P.M. She relaxes for 55 minutes before she goes to aerobics class. What time does she leave for class? _____

4. Carol put a turkey in the oven at 9:25 A.M. The turkey cooked for 5 hours. What time did she take the turkey out of the oven? _____

5. Richard left Newark Airport at 9:55 P.M. His flight to Miami took 2 hours 10 minutes. What time did he arrive in Miami? _____

6. Justin began his shift at 10:35 P.M. He worked for 7 hours. What time did Justin get off work? _____

7. Eleanor begins her lunch hour at 11:45 A.M. She leaves work at 4:45 P.M. How long is it between the start of lunch and the end of the work day? _____

CHAPTER 19

Customary Units of Length

The most commonly used customary units of length are the **inch** (in.), the **foot** (ft), the **yard** (yd), and the **mile** (mi).

12 inches	=	1 foot
3 feet	=	1 yard
5,280 feet	=	1 mile
1,760 yards	=	1 mile

We use inches to measure small objects.
We use miles to measure long distances.

Example: Which is the better unit to measure:

a. width of a room?	ft
b. distance to work?	mi
c. length of fabric?	yd
d. an index finger?	in.

MENTAL MATH

You can compare units of length mentally.

Which is greater, 15 in. or 1 ft?

Think: 1 ft = 12 in.

So, 15 in. is greater than 1 ft.

Example: Which is greater, 3 yd or 13 ft? Compare.

Think: 3 yd = 9 ft.

So, 13 ft is greater than 3 yd.

Example: Brittany jogged 6 miles in 1 hour. How many yards is that?

To change a larger unit to a smaller unit, multiply.

$$
\begin{aligned}
6 \text{ mi} &= \text{? yd} \\
1 \text{ mi} &= 1{,}760 \text{ yd} \\
6 \times 1{,}760 &= 10{,}560 \\
6 \text{ mi} &= 10{,}560 \text{ yd}
\end{aligned}
$$

Brittany jogged 10,560 yd.

Example: Danny measured the window in his bathroom for new curtains. The window is 48 in. wide. How many feet is the window?

To change a smaller unit to a larger unit, divide.

$$
\begin{aligned}
48 \text{ in.} &= \text{? ft} \\
12 \text{ in.} &= 1 \text{ ft} \\
48 \div 12 &= 4 \\
48 \text{ in.} &= 4 \text{ ft}
\end{aligned}
$$

The window is 4 ft wide.

Example: Mary has a piece of fabric that is 4 ft 5 in. wide. How many inches wide is the fabric?

$$
\begin{aligned}
4 \text{ ft } 5 \text{ in.} &= \text{? in.} \\
1 \text{ ft} &= 12 \text{ in.} \\
4 \times 12 &= 48 \\
48 + 5 &= 53 \\
4 \text{ ft } 5 \text{ in.} &= 53 \text{ in.}
\end{aligned}
$$

The fabric is 53 in. wide.

Exercise 19-A

Choose the better unit to measure each of the following.

1. distance around your hips   a. yd   b. ft   c. in.

2. width of a notebook   a. mi   b. ft   c. in.

3. distance to the airport   a. yd   b. mi   c. in.

4. height of a building   a. ft   b. in.   c. mi

5. length of a football field   a. in.   b. ft   c. mi

Exercise 19-B

Complete.

6. 36 in. = _____ ft   7. 60 ft = _____ yd   8. 108 in. = _____ ft

9. 10,560 ft = _____ mi   10. 300 ft = _____ yd   11. 27 ft = _____ yd

12. 72 in. = _____ yd   13. _____ in. = 4 ft   14. _____ ft = 144 in.

15. 252 in. = _____ yd   16. _____ ft = 180 in.   17. 60 in. = _____ ft

18. 84 in. = _____ ft   19. _____ ft = 1 mi   20. 3 mi = _____ yd

21. 2 ft 4 in. = _____ in.   22. 16 ft = _____ yd _____ ft

23. 5 ft 8 in. = _____ in.   24. 2,000 yd = _____ mi _____ yd

25. 9 yd 2 ft = _____ ft   26. 7 ft 8 in. = _____ in.

CHAPTER 20

Customary Units of Weight and Capacity

To measure weight we usually use customary units of weight such as the **ounce** (oz), the **pound** (lb), and the **ton** (T).

> 16 ounces   =   1 pound
> 2,000 pounds =   1 ton

We use ounces to measure light objects.
We use pounds and tons to measure heavy objects.

Example: Which is the better unit to measure:

    a. a horse?   lb
    b. a kitten?   lb
    c. an onion?   oz
    d. a moving truck? T

Example: Roger buys 2 lb of green peppers at the grocery store. How many ounces is that?

To change from a larger unit to a smaller unit, multiply.

$$2 \text{ lb} = ? \text{ oz}$$
$$1 \text{ lb} = 16 \text{ oz}$$
$$2 \times 16 = 32$$
$$2 \text{ lb} = 32 \text{ oz}$$

Roger buys 32 oz of green peppers.

Example: 80 oz = ? lb

To change from a smaller unit to a larger unit, divide.

$$80 \text{ oz} = ? \text{ lb}$$
$$16 \text{ oz} = 1 \text{ lb}$$
$$80 \div 16 = 5$$
$$80 \text{ oz} = 5 \text{ lb}$$

To measure capacity we usually use customary units such as the **fluid ounce** (fl oz), the **cup** (c), the **pint** (pt), the **quart** (qt), and the **gallon** (gal).

8 fluid ounces	=	1 cup
2 cups	=	1 pint
2 pints	=	1 quart
4 quarts	=	1 gallon

We use cups to measure small quantities of liquids. We use gallons to measure larger quantities of liquids.

Example: Which is the better unit to measure:

a. paint?   gal
b. motor oil?   qt
c. water in a bathtub?   gal
d. a juice glass?   c

Example: Ashley buys 2 gallons of apple cider. How many quarts is that?

To change from a larger unit to a smaller unit, multiply.

$$2 \text{ gal} = ? \text{ qt}$$
$$1 \text{ gal} = 4 \text{ qt}$$
$$2 \times 4 = 8$$
$$2 \text{ gal} = 8 \text{ qt}$$

Ashley buys 8 qt of apple cider.

Example: 16 pt = ? qt

To change from a smaller unit to a larger unit, divide.

$$16 \text{ pt} = ? \text{ qt}$$
$$2 \text{ pt} = 1 \text{ qt}$$
$$16 \div 2 = 8$$
$$16 \text{ pt} = 8 \text{ qt}$$

Exercise 20-A

Complete.

1. Mel weighs about 195 _____.

2. A small carton of juice holds about 1 _____.

3. An envelope weighs about 1 _____.

4. A washing machine holds about 50 _____ of water.

5. Jan used about 2 _____ of paint in the living room.

Exercise 20-B

Complete.

6. 10 c = _____ pt

7. 8 lb = _____ oz

8. 2 T = _____ lb

9. 6 pt = _____ c

10. _____ fl oz = 3 c

11. 32 pt = _____ qt

12. 15 lb = _____ oz

13. 40 oz = _____ pt

14. 14 pt = _____ qt

15. _____ fl oz = 3 c

16. _____ oz = 9 lb

17. _____ gal = 8 qt

18. _____ gal = 10 qt

19. _____ fl oz = 1 c

20. _____ T = 6,500 lb

21. 4 lb 10 oz = _____ oz

22. 3 T 62 lb = _____ lb

23. 13 pt = _____ qt _____ pt

24. 4 gal 1 qt = _____ qt

25. 100 oz = _____ lb _____ oz

26. 1,000 lb = _____ T

CHAPTER 21

Temperature

The weather bureau gives the outside temperature in **degrees Fahrenheit**, a customary unit of measure.

Look at the thermometer.

The temperature of Pat's tea is 54°F below the temperature of boiling water. What is the temperature of the tea?

To find the difference, subtract 54°F from 212°F.

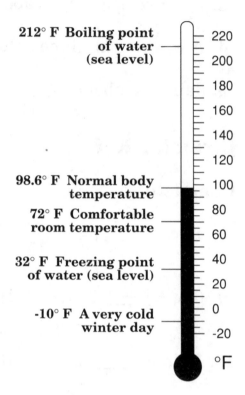

212° F Boiling point of water (sea level)

98.6° F Normal body temperature

72° F Comfortable room temperature

32° F Freezing point of water (sea level)

-10° F A very cold winter day

°F

$$\begin{array}{r} 212 \\ -\ 54 \\ \hline 158 \end{array}$$

Pat's tea is 158°F.

Example: The outside temperature on Saturday was 13°F below the freezing point of water. What was the temperature?

To find out, look at the thermometer. Subtract 13°F from 32°F.

$$\begin{array}{r} 32 \\ -\ 13 \\ \hline 19 \end{array}$$

It was 19°F on Saturday.

Exercise 21-A

Write the temperature.

1.

_____

2.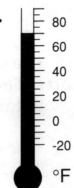

_____

3.

_____

4.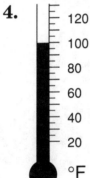

_____

5.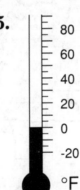

_____

6.

_____

Exercise 21-B

Choose the most reasonable temperature.

7. hot soup   a. 30°F   b. 75°F   c. 110°F

8. a summer day   a. 85°F   b. −10°F   c. 45°F

9. an autumn day   a. 92°F   b. 61°F   c. 25°F

10. baking potatoes   a. 30°F   b. 400°F   c. 90°F

11. ice cubes   a. 40°F   b. 31°F   c. 60°F

APPLICATION

Time Zones

There are four standard time zones in the Continental United States. They are Eastern (EST), Central (CST), Mountain (MST), and Pacific (PST).

When it is 6:00 P.M. in Kansas City, what time is it in each city?

1. Dallas _____

2. San Francisco _____

3. Seattle _____

4. Chicago _____

5. New Orleans _____

6. Miami _____

7. Buffalo _____

8. Denver _____

9. Phoenix _____

A newscast is being shown live from Seattle at 11:00 P.M. What time is it being seen in each city?

10. Kansas City _____

11. Pittsburgh _____

12. Miami _____

13. Minneapolis _____

14. New York _____

15. Atlanta _____

$\mathcal{Q}$uiz for **UNIT 3**

Complete.

1. _____ s = 7 min

2. 192 h = _____ d

3. 156 wk = _____ y

4. 6 d = _____ h

5. 1 d = _____ min

6. 540 min = _____ h

7. 48 in. = _____ ft

8. _____ ft = 1 yd

9. 3 mi = _____ ft

10. _____ yd = 1 mi

11. 12 ft = _____ yd

12. _____ in. = 8 ft

13. 80 oz = _____ lb

14. _____ lb = 4 T

15. 9 lb = _____ oz

16. _____ fl oz = 1 c

17. 4 pt = _____ qt

18. 1 gal = _____ qt

19. 16 c = _____ pt

20. 40 qt = _____ gal

21. _____ pt = 2 qt

Add or subtract.

22.   6 h 12 min
   + 3 h 15 min

23.   13 h 40 min
   + 3 h 50 min

24.   8 min 31 s
  − 3 min 45 s

25.   10 h   5 min
  − 8 h 33 min

Solve.

26. Katie gets up at 6:45 A.M. She has to leave for
work at 9:00 A.M. How long does she have to
get ready for work?

_____

CUMULATIVE REVIEW

Circle the letter of the correct answer.

Add or subtract.

1. 3.09 + 4.98
   - a. 8.7
   - b. 8.07
   - c. 0.807
   - d. none of these

2. 13 – 8.2
   - a. 4.8
   - b. 4
   - c. 5
   - d. none of these

3. 6.9 + 4.89
   - a. 11.7
   - b. 11.9
   - c. 1.179
   - d. none of these

Multiply or divide.

4. 0.9 x 114.8
   - a. 103.32
   - b. 1,033.2
   - c. 10.332
   - d. none of these

5. 60.94 ÷ 100
   - a. 6.094
   - b. 0.06094
   - c. 0.6094
   - d. none of these

6. $12.43 x 812
   - a. $10,093.16
   - b. $100.93
   - c. $1,093.16
   - d. none of these

Complete.

7. 120 s = ___?___ min
   - a. 2
   - b. 7,200
   - c. 20
   - d. none of these

8. ___?___ in. = 12 ft
   - a. 4
   - b. 96
   - c. 144
   - d. none of these

9. 24 fl oz = ___?___ c
   - a. 8
   - b. 16
   - c. 3
   - d. none of these

10. Which unit would you use to find your belt size?
    - a. ft
    - b. in.
    - c. yd
    - d. none of these

11. Which unit would you use to measure a bag of flour?
    - a. T
    - b. lb
    - c. oz
    - d. none of these

Add or subtract.

12. 16 h 4 min + 4 h 59 min
    - a. 20 h 63 min
    - b. 21 h 3 min
    - c. 21 h
    - d. none of these

13. 5 min 12 s – 2 min 42 s
    - a. 2 h 22 min
    - b. 3 h 30 min
    - c. 2 h 30 min
    - d. none of these

14. Donna called her son at 9:20 P.M. She talked for 40 minutes. What time did she get off the phone?
    - a. 9:00 P.M.
    - b. 10:00 P.M.
    - c. 10:05 P.M.
    - d. none of these

Adding and Subtracting Fractions

Ralph's stock in the company rose $1\frac{7}{8}$ points last month and $3\frac{1}{4}$ points this month. How much did the stock rise altogether?

CHAPTER 22

Fractions

Paula shops at Katy's Kitchen. She buys a magnet to put on her dishwasher so her family knows if the dishes inside are clean or dirty. She buys the magnet with one half shaded. Which magnet did she buy?

Magnet 1   **Magnet 2**   **Magnet 3**

Paula chose Magnet 2. This magnet has 2 equal parts or 2 halves. One half is shaded.

A **fraction** names part of a region or part of a group. You write the fraction one half as $\frac{1}{2}$.

$\frac{1}{2}$ ← The **numerator** is the number of parts shaded.
← The **denominator** is the total number of equal parts.

Example: Jerry ate 3 pieces of cherry pie. What fraction of the pie did Jerry eat?

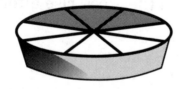

The numerator is the number of pieces of pie that Jerry ate, 3.

The denominator is the total number of pieces in the whole pie, 8.

Jerry ate $\frac{3}{8}$ of the pie.

A fraction names part of a group.

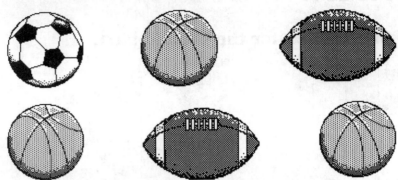

Of the 6 balls, 2 are footballs.
Two sixths of the balls are footballs.

Write: $\frac{2}{6}$

Of the 6 balls, 3 are basketballs.
Three sixths of the balls are basketballs.

Write: $\frac{3}{6}$

Example: Dan coaches his son's little league team. There are 10 players on the team. Three of the players bat left-handed. What fraction of the players bat left-handed? What fraction of the players bat right-handed?

Three out of 10 players bat left-handed, so three tenths of the players bat left-handed.

Write: $\frac{3}{10}$

Seven out of the 10 players are right-handed, so seven tenths of the players bat right-handed.

Write: $\frac{7}{10}$

Exercise 22-A

Write the fraction for the shaded part.

1.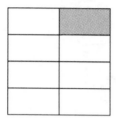

2.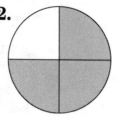

3.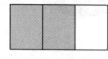

4.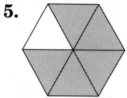

5.

6.

Exercise 22-B

What fraction is shaded?

7.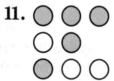

8.

9.

10.

11.

12.

Exercise 22-C

Write the fraction.

13. two thirds _____

14. one fifth _____

15. seven eighths _____

16. one half _____

17. three fourths _____

18. nine tenths _____

Exercise 22-D

Complete.

19.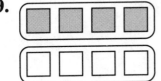

$\frac{1}{2}$ are shaded.

$\frac{1}{2}$ of 8 is _____ .

20.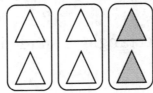

$\frac{1}{3}$ are shaded.

$\frac{1}{3}$ of 6 is _____ .

21.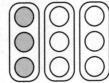

$\frac{1}{3}$ are shaded.

$\frac{1}{3}$ of 9 is _____ .

22.

$\frac{1}{3}$ are shaded.

$\frac{1}{3}$ of 12 is _____ .

23.

$\frac{1}{4}$ are shaded.

$\frac{1}{4}$ of 12 is _____ .

24.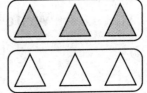

$\frac{1}{2}$ are shaded.

$\frac{1}{2}$ of 6 is _____ .

CHAPTER 23

Equivalent Fractions

This rectangle is divided into 4 equal parts.

$\frac{1}{4}$	$\frac{1}{4}$	$\frac{1}{4}$	$\frac{1}{4}$

$\frac{1}{4}$ of the rectangle is shaded.

This rectangle is divided into 8 equal parts.

$\frac{1}{8}$	$\frac{1}{8}$	$\frac{1}{8}$	$\frac{1}{8}$	$\frac{1}{8}$	$\frac{1}{8}$	$\frac{1}{8}$	$\frac{1}{8}$

$\frac{2}{8}$ of the rectangle is shaded.

Look at both rectangles. You can see that $\frac{1}{4}$ and $\frac{2}{8}$ are the same size.

$\frac{1}{4}$ and $\frac{2}{8}$ are **equivalent fractions**.

Example: Write an equivalent fraction.

$\frac{1}{6}$	$\frac{1}{6}$	$\frac{1}{6}$	$\frac{1}{6}$	$\frac{1}{6}$	$\frac{1}{6}$

$\frac{1}{12}$	$\frac{1}{12}$	$\frac{1}{12}$	$\frac{1}{12}$	$\frac{1}{12}$	$\frac{1}{12}$	$\frac{1}{12}$	$\frac{1}{12}$	$\frac{1}{12}$	$\frac{1}{12}$	$\frac{1}{12}$	$\frac{1}{12}$

You can also find equivalent fractions by multiplying the numerator and the denominator by the same number, except zero.

$$\frac{2}{6} = \frac{2 \times 2}{6 \times 2} = \frac{4}{12}$$

Exercise 23-A

Write a number sentence to show equivalent fractions.

1.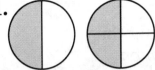

_____

2.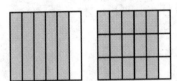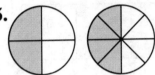

_____

3.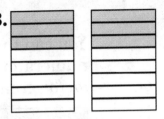

_____

4.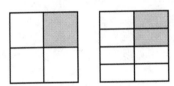

_____

5.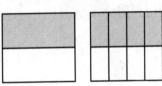

_____

6.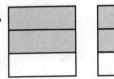

_____

7.

_____

8.

_____

9.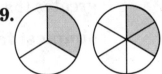

_____

Exercise 23-B

Write the equivalent fraction.

10. $\dfrac{1}{6} = \dfrac{1 \times 2}{6 \times 2} = $ _____

11. $\dfrac{1}{2} = \dfrac{1 \times 6}{2 \times 6} = $ _____

12. $\dfrac{1}{8} = \dfrac{1 \times 4}{8 \times 4} = $ _____

13. $\dfrac{3}{7} = \dfrac{3 \times 2}{7 \times 2} = $ _____

14. $\dfrac{3}{10} = \dfrac{3 \times 5}{10 \times 5} = $ _____

15. $\dfrac{1}{7} = \dfrac{1 \times 2}{7 \times 2} = $ _____

16. $\dfrac{2}{9} = \dfrac{2 \times 2}{9 \times 2} = $ _____

17. $\dfrac{5}{6} = \dfrac{5 \times 3}{6 \times 3} = $ _____

18. $\dfrac{6}{7} = \dfrac{6 \times 4}{7 \times 4} = $ _____

CHAPTER 24

Simplest Form

You can find equivalent fractions by dividing the numerator and the denominator by a *common factor* greater than one.

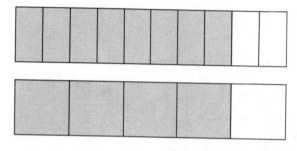

$$\frac{8}{10} = \frac{8 \div 2}{10 \div 2} = \frac{4}{5}$$

The numerator and the denominator of the fraction $\frac{4}{5}$ cannot be divided by a common factor greater than one. The fraction $\frac{4}{5}$ is in **simplest form.**

Example: Write the fraction in simplest form.

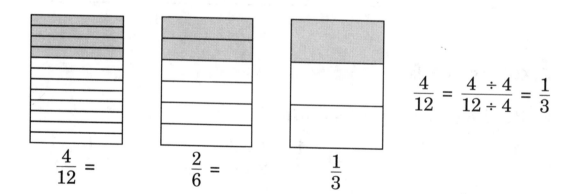

$$\frac{4}{12} = \qquad \frac{2}{6} = \qquad \frac{1}{3}$$

$$\frac{4}{12} = \frac{4 \div 4}{12 \div 4} = \frac{1}{3}$$

Example: Write $\frac{5}{5}$ in simplest form.

If the numerator and the denominator are the same number, the fraction is equal to 1.

$$\frac{5}{5} = \frac{5 \div 5}{5 \div 5} = \frac{1}{1} = 1$$

1.

$$\frac{2}{4} = \frac{\boxed{}}{\boxed{}}$$

2.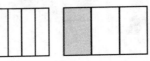

$$\frac{2}{6} = \frac{\boxed{}}{\boxed{}}$$

3.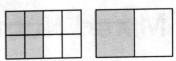

$$\frac{4}{8} = \frac{\boxed{}}{\boxed{}}$$

Exercise 24-B

Complete.

4. $\dfrac{3}{9} = \dfrac{3 \div 3}{9 \div 3} = $ _____

5. $\dfrac{10}{15} = \dfrac{10 \div 5}{15 \div 5} = $ _____

6. $\dfrac{4}{10} = \dfrac{4 \div 2}{10 \div 2} = $ _____

7. $\dfrac{6}{8} = \dfrac{6 \div 2}{8 \div 2} = $ _____

8. $\dfrac{5}{20} = \dfrac{5 \div 5}{20 \div 5} = $ _____

9. $\dfrac{8}{12} = \dfrac{8 \div 4}{12 \div 4} = $ _____

10. $\dfrac{12}{24} = \dfrac{12 \div 12}{24 \div 12} = $ _____

11. $\dfrac{7}{14} = \dfrac{7 \div 7}{14 \div 7} = $ _____

12. $\dfrac{8}{8} = \dfrac{8 \div 8}{8 \div 8} = $ _____

Exercise 24-C

M

MENTAL MATH

Complete.

13. $\dfrac{8}{16} = \dfrac{\boxed{}}{2}$

14. $\dfrac{4}{16} = \dfrac{\boxed{}}{4}$

15. $\dfrac{7}{28} = \dfrac{1}{\boxed{}}$

16. $\dfrac{8}{20} = \dfrac{\boxed{}}{5}$

17. $\dfrac{2}{10} = \dfrac{1}{\boxed{}}$

18. $\dfrac{3}{15} = \dfrac{\boxed{}}{5}$

CHAPTER 25

Mixed Numbers

Sometimes the numerator of a fraction is greater than the denominator. When this happens, the fraction is greater than 1. A fraction greater than 1 is called a **mixed number**.

Look at the diagram.

$$\frac{3}{3} \qquad\qquad \frac{1}{3}$$

Write the fraction for the shaded parts. $\frac{4}{3}$

Since the numerator 4 is greater than 3, we can write a mixed number.

One whole rectangle is shaded and one third of the other rectangle is shaded.

We write the mixed number as $1\frac{1}{3}$.

Example: Write $\frac{7}{4}$ as a mixed number.

You can write a fraction as a mixed number by dividing the numerator by the denominator.

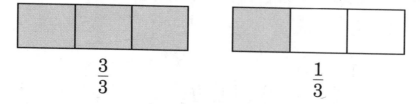

The remainder becomes the numerator.
The divisor becomes the denominator.

Sometimes a fraction names a whole number with no remainders.

$$\frac{6}{3} \;\rightarrow\; 3\overline{)6}^{\,2} \;\rightarrow\; \frac{6}{3} = 2$$

Exercise 25-A

Write the fraction as a mixed number in simplest form or as a whole number.

1.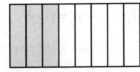

$$\frac{11}{8} = \underline{\hspace{2cm}}$$

2.

$$\frac{15}{6} = \underline{\hspace{2cm}}$$

3.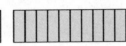

$$\frac{20}{10} = \underline{\hspace{2cm}}$$

4.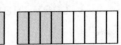

$$\frac{13}{9} = \underline{\hspace{2cm}}$$

Exercise 25-B

Write the fraction as a whole number.

5. $\frac{20}{5} = \underline{\hspace{1.5cm}}$ 6. $\frac{14}{7} = \underline{\hspace{1.5cm}}$ 7. $\frac{40}{8} = \underline{\hspace{1.5cm}}$ 8. $\frac{35}{7} = \underline{\hspace{1.5cm}}$

Exercise 25-C

Write the fraction as a mixed number in simplest form.

9. $\frac{8}{5} = \underline{\hspace{1cm}}$ 10. $\frac{11}{5} = \underline{\hspace{1cm}}$ 11. $\frac{10}{3} = \underline{\hspace{1cm}}$ 12. $\frac{20}{6} = \underline{\hspace{1cm}}$

13. $\frac{22}{9} = \underline{\hspace{1cm}}$ 14. $\frac{13}{7} = \underline{\hspace{1cm}}$ 15. $\frac{14}{4} = \underline{\hspace{1cm}}$ 16. $\frac{12}{8} = \underline{\hspace{1cm}}$

Exercise 25-D

Solve.

17. Yolanda needs 16 grapefruit halves to serve to her guests. How many grapefruits does she need?   _____

18. Ricky picked 22 peaches. Each small carton holds 6 peaches. Write a mixed number to show how many cartons Ricky filled with peaches.   _____

CHAPTER 26

Adding Fractions with Like Denominators

Bill and Ted are working on the company newsletter. They want $\frac{1}{6}$ of the newsletter to be on new employees and $\frac{4}{6}$ of the newsletter to be on new policies. How much of the newsletter have they planned so far?

To find out, add the fractions.

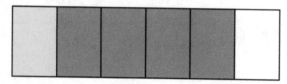

one sixth + four sixths = five sixths

To add fractions with like denominators, add the numerators. Write the sum over the same or like denominator. Remember, always write the sum in simplest form.

| Keep the same denominator. | $\dfrac{1}{6} + \dfrac{4}{6} = \dfrac{5}{6}$ | Add the numerators. |

Add $\frac{1}{8} + \frac{3}{8}$. Write the sum in simplest form.

$$\frac{1}{8} + \frac{3}{8} = \frac{4}{8} = \frac{1}{2}$$ Write the sum in simplest form.

Example: Danielle is using a recipe that calls for $\frac{1}{3}$ cup of flour. She wants to double it for high altitude baking. How much flour does she need?

To find out, add the fractions.

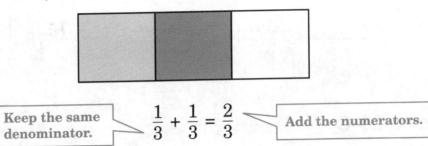

Keep the same denominator.

$\frac{1}{3} + \frac{1}{3} = \frac{2}{3}$

Add the numerators.

Danielle needs $\frac{2}{3}$ cup of flour.

Exercise 26-A

Add. Write the sum in simplest form.

1.

$\frac{1}{4} + \frac{2}{4} = $ _____

2.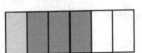

$\frac{1}{6} + \frac{3}{6} = $ _____

3.

$\frac{2}{7} + \frac{1}{7} = $ _____

4.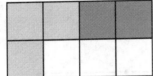

$\frac{3}{8} + \frac{2}{8} = $ _____

5.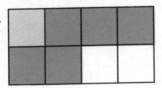

$\frac{1}{8} + \frac{5}{8} = $ _____

6.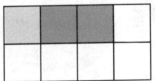

$\frac{1}{8} + \frac{2}{8} = $ _____

7.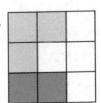

$\frac{3}{9} + \frac{2}{9} = $ _____

8.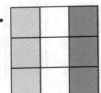

$\frac{3}{9} + \frac{3}{9} = $ _____

9.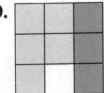

$\frac{5}{9} + \frac{3}{9} = $ _____

Exercise 26-B

Add. Write the sum in simplest form.

10. $\frac{1}{3} + \frac{2}{3} =$ _____

11. $\frac{2}{8} + \frac{4}{8} =$ _____

12. $\frac{1}{8} + \frac{6}{8} =$ _____

13. $\frac{5}{12} + \frac{3}{12} =$ _____

14. $\frac{1}{10} + \frac{4}{10} =$ _____

15. $\frac{3}{9} + \frac{4}{9} =$ _____

Exercise 26-C

Solve.

16. Jessica ate $\frac{1}{8}$ of the apple pie on Monday. Roger ate $\frac{2}{8}$ of the pie on Tuesday. How much of the pie did they eat?

_____

17. Rosa walked $\frac{3}{10}$ mi on Saturday and $\frac{5}{10}$ mi on Sunday. How far did Rosa walk altogether?

_____

 ENTAL MATH

Add the fraction in the middle to each fraction in the outer ring. Use mental math. Write each sum in simplest form.

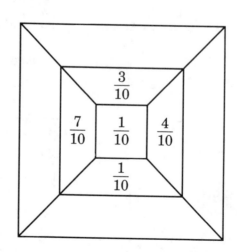

CHAPTER 27

Subtracting Fractions with Like Denominators

Betty buys a piece of ribbon that is $\frac{7}{10}$ yd long.

She uses $\frac{3}{10}$ of the ribbon. How much ribbon does she have left? To find out, subtract.

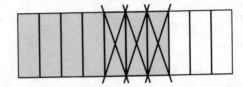

To subtract fractions with the same denominators, subtract the numerators. Write the difference over the same denominator. Remember to write the difference in simplest form.

$$\begin{array}{r} \frac{7}{10} \\ -\frac{3}{10} \\ \hline 4 \end{array}$$ Subtract the numerators. $7 - 3 = 4$

$$\begin{array}{r} \frac{7}{10} \\ -\frac{3}{10} \\ \hline \frac{4}{10} \end{array}$$ Write the same denominator.

$$\begin{array}{r} \frac{7}{10} \\ -\frac{3}{10} \\ \hline \frac{4}{10} = \frac{2}{5} \end{array}$$ Write in simplest form.

Betty has $\frac{2}{5}$ yd of ribbon left.

Subtract: $\frac{12}{16} - \frac{6}{16}$. Write the difference in simplest form.

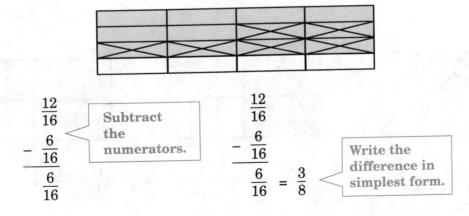

$$\begin{array}{r} \frac{12}{16} \\ -\frac{6}{16} \\ \hline \frac{6}{16} \end{array}$$ Subtract the numerators.

$$\begin{array}{r} \frac{12}{16} \\ -\frac{6}{16} \\ \hline \frac{6}{16} = \frac{3}{8} \end{array}$$ Write the difference in simplest form.

Example: Marcy uses $\frac{7}{8}$ of her backyard for a vegetable garden. She plants tomatoes in $\frac{3}{8}$ of the garden.

How much room does she have left in her backyard to plant other vegetables?

To find out, subtract.

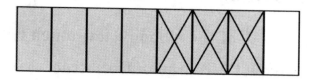

Keep the same denominator.

$$\frac{7}{8} - \frac{3}{8} = \frac{4}{8} = \frac{2}{4} = \frac{1}{2}$$

Subtract the numerators. Then simplify.

Exercise 27-A

Subtract. Write the difference in simplest form.

1.
$$\begin{array}{r} \frac{4}{10} \\ -\ \frac{2}{10} \\ \hline \end{array}$$
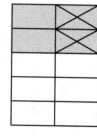

2.
$$\begin{array}{r} \frac{8}{9} \\ -\ \frac{2}{9} \\ \hline \end{array}$$
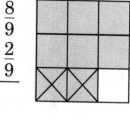

3.
$$\begin{array}{r} \frac{3}{4} \\ -\ \frac{2}{4} \\ \hline \end{array}$$

4.
$$\begin{array}{r} \frac{5}{8} \\ -\ \frac{1}{8} \\ \hline \end{array}$$

5.
$$\begin{array}{r} \frac{11}{12} \\ -\ \frac{3}{12} \\ \hline \end{array}$$

6.
$$\begin{array}{r} \frac{11}{16} \\ -\ \frac{7}{16} \\ \hline \end{array}$$
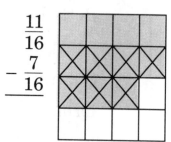

7.

$$\frac{4}{5} - \frac{2}{5} = \underline{\hspace{1cm}}$$

8.
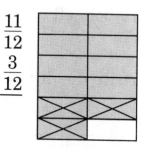

$$\frac{9}{12} - \frac{4}{12} = \underline{\hspace{1cm}}$$

9.
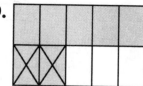

$$\frac{7}{10} - \frac{2}{10} = \underline{\hspace{1cm}}$$

Subtract. Write the difference in simplest form.

10. $\dfrac{4}{5} - \dfrac{2}{5} =$ _____

11. $\dfrac{5}{6} - \dfrac{2}{6} =$ _____

12. $\dfrac{7}{12} - \dfrac{2}{12} =$ _____

13. $\dfrac{10}{12} - \dfrac{2}{12} =$ _____

14. $\dfrac{8}{15} - \dfrac{3}{15} =$ _____

15. $\dfrac{15}{16} - \dfrac{9}{16} =$ _____

Exercise 27-C

Solve.

16. Joanne walked $\dfrac{11}{12}$ mi on Monday and $\dfrac{5}{12}$ mi on Tuesday. How much farther did she walk on Monday?

_____

17. Barry's stock rose $\dfrac{7}{16}$ on Thursday and $\dfrac{11}{16}$ on Friday. How much more did his stock rise on Friday than on Thursday?

_____

18. Katy has a piece of embroidery thread that is $\dfrac{7}{12}$ in. long. She cuts the thread into two pieces. One piece measures $\dfrac{3}{12}$ in. long. What is the length of the other piece?

_____

CHAPTER 28

Comparing Fractions

You can compare fractions using a number line.

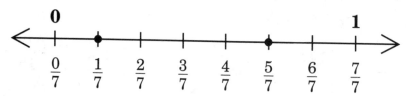

Compare $\frac{1}{7}$ and $\frac{5}{7}$. Since the denominators are the same, compare the numerators.

$$1 < 5, \text{ so } \frac{1}{7} < \frac{5}{7}$$

Example: Compare $\frac{1}{4}$ and $\frac{3}{8}$.

Since the denominators are not the same, write an equivalent fraction.

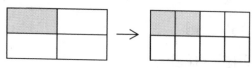

$$\frac{1}{4} = \frac{1 \times 2}{4 \times 2} = \frac{2}{8} \qquad\qquad \frac{3}{8}$$

Now compare. $\frac{2}{8} < \frac{3}{8}$ so $\frac{1}{4} < \frac{3}{8}$.

Is $\frac{6}{7}$ closer to 1, $\frac{1}{2}$, or 0?

ESTIMATING

You can estimate that $\frac{6}{7}$ is close to 1 because the numerator is almost as great as the denominator. $\frac{7}{12}$ is close to $\frac{1}{2}$ because the denominator is about twice the numerator.

$\frac{1}{16}$ is close to 0 because the numerator is so much less than the denominator.

Exercise 28-A

Compare. Write <, >, or =.

1.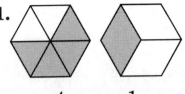

$$\frac{4}{6} \underline{\hspace{1cm}} \frac{1}{3}$$

2.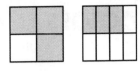

$$\frac{3}{4} \underline{\hspace{1cm}} \frac{3}{8}$$

3.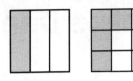

$$\frac{1}{3} \underline{\hspace{1cm}} \frac{4}{9}$$

Exercise 28-B

Compare. Write <, >, or =. Use the number line.

4. $\frac{2}{6} \underline{\hspace{1cm}} \frac{1}{3}$ **5.** $\frac{5}{6} \underline{\hspace{1cm}} \frac{2}{3}$

6. $\frac{1}{2} \underline{\hspace{1cm}} \frac{1}{6}$ **7.** $\frac{1}{3} \underline{\hspace{1cm}} \frac{6}{6}$

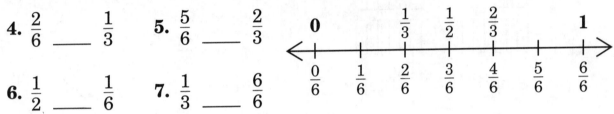

Exercise 28-C

Compare. Write <, >, or =.

8. $\frac{3}{4} \underline{\hspace{1cm}} \frac{1}{8}$ **9.** $\frac{2}{3} \underline{\hspace{1cm}} \frac{5}{6}$ **10.** $\frac{5}{9} \underline{\hspace{1cm}} \frac{1}{3}$ **11.** $\frac{1}{2} \underline{\hspace{1cm}} \frac{7}{8}$

12. $\frac{5}{20} \underline{\hspace{1cm}} \frac{10}{15}$ **13.** $\frac{3}{5} \underline{\hspace{1cm}} \frac{4}{10}$ **14.** $\frac{2}{4} \underline{\hspace{1cm}} \frac{4}{8}$ **15.** $\frac{6}{7} \underline{\hspace{1cm}} \frac{8}{14}$

ESTIMATING

Estimate. Tell whether the fraction is about 1, $\frac{1}{2}$, or 0.

16. $\frac{8}{9} \underline{\hspace{1cm}}$ **17.** $\frac{1}{3} \underline{\hspace{1cm}}$ **18.** $\frac{1}{12} \underline{\hspace{1cm}}$ **19.** $\frac{6}{7} \underline{\hspace{1cm}}$

20. $\frac{5}{8} \underline{\hspace{1cm}}$ **21.** $\frac{3}{4} \underline{\hspace{1cm}}$ **22.** $\frac{11}{12} \underline{\hspace{1cm}}$ **23.** $\frac{7}{12} \underline{\hspace{1cm}}$

CHAPTER 29

Adding Fractions with Unlike Denominators

Mike made a tape of his favorite songs. One half of the tape contains dance music and $\frac{1}{6}$ of the tape contains rock music. What part of the tape has he used so far?

To find out, add.

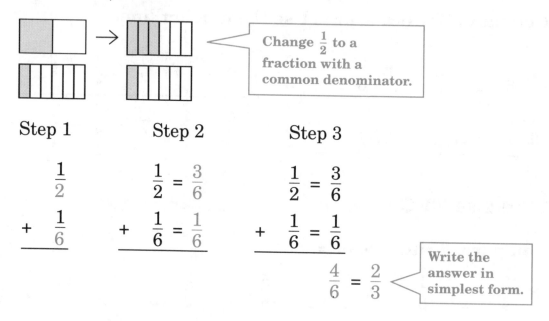

Change $\frac{1}{2}$ to a fraction with a common denominator.

Step 1

$$\frac{1}{2}$$
$$+ \frac{1}{6}$$

Step 2

$$\frac{1}{2} = \frac{3}{6}$$
$$+ \frac{1}{6} = \frac{1}{6}$$

Step 3

$$\frac{1}{2} = \frac{3}{6}$$
$$+ \frac{1}{6} = \frac{1}{6}$$
$$\frac{4}{6} = \frac{2}{3}$$

Write the answer in simplest form.

Example: Add $\frac{4}{5}$ and $\frac{3}{10}$.

Step 1

$$\frac{4}{5}$$
$$+ \frac{3}{10}$$

Step 2

$$\frac{4}{5} = \frac{8}{10}$$
$$+ \frac{3}{10} = \frac{3}{10}$$

Step 3

$$\frac{4}{5} = \frac{8}{10}$$
$$+ \frac{3}{10} = \frac{3}{10}$$
$$\frac{11}{10} = 1\frac{1}{10}$$

Write the answer in simplest form.

You can only add fractions when you have a common denominator.

Example: Add $1\frac{1}{3} + 3\frac{3}{6}$.

Step 1

$$1\frac{1}{3}$$
$$+\,3\frac{3}{6}$$

Step 2

$$1\frac{1}{3} = 1\frac{2}{6}$$
$$+\,3\frac{3}{6} = 3\frac{3}{6}$$
$$\overline{\qquad\;\; 4\frac{5}{6}}$$

Step 1   Write the fraction with a common denominator.

Step 2   Add the fractions. Then add the whole numbers.

Example: Ernie bought $2\frac{3}{4}$ gal of gas on Tuesday and $8\frac{2}{3}$ gal on Saturday. How much gas did he buy in all?

To find out, add.

Step 1

$$2\frac{3}{4} = \frac{3 \times 3}{4 \times 3} = \frac{9}{12}$$
$$+\,8\frac{2}{3} = \frac{2 \times 4}{3 \times 4} = \frac{8}{12}$$

Step 2

$$2\frac{3}{4} = 2\frac{9}{12}$$
$$+\,8\frac{2}{3} = 8\frac{8}{12}$$
$$\overline{\qquad\quad 10\frac{17}{12}}$$

Step 3

$$10\frac{17}{12} = 10 + 1\frac{5}{12} = 11\frac{5}{12}$$

Step 1   Write fractions with a common denominator.

Step 2   Add the fractions. Then add the whole numbers.

Step 3   Rename $\frac{17}{12}$ to a mixed number. Write the sum in simplest form.

Ernie bought $11\frac{5}{12}$ gal of gas.

Exercise 29-A

1. $\frac{1}{3} = \frac{\square}{6}$

2. $\frac{1}{4} = \frac{2}{\square}$

3. $\frac{1}{6} = \frac{3}{\square}$

4. $\frac{2}{5} = \frac{\square}{10}$

5. $2\frac{2}{3} = 2\frac{\square}{6}$

6. $4\frac{6}{5} = 5\frac{\square}{5}$

7. $6\frac{5}{6} = 6\frac{10}{\square}$

8. $1\frac{10}{9} = 2\frac{1}{\square}$

Exercise 29-B

Add. Write the sum in simplest form.

9. $\begin{array}{r} \frac{3}{4} \\ + \frac{3}{8} \\ \hline \end{array}$

10. $\begin{array}{r} \frac{3}{10} \\ + \frac{1}{5} \\ \hline \end{array}$

11. $\begin{array}{r} \frac{1}{12} \\ + \frac{2}{3} \\ \hline \end{array}$

12. $\begin{array}{r} \frac{5}{12} \\ + \frac{1}{3} \\ \hline \end{array}$

13. $\begin{array}{r} \frac{2}{5} \\ + \frac{7}{10} \\ \hline \end{array}$

14. $\begin{array}{r} \frac{7}{8} \\ + \frac{1}{4} \\ \hline \end{array}$

15. $\begin{array}{r} \frac{5}{6} \\ + \frac{2}{3} \\ \hline \end{array}$

16. $\begin{array}{r} \frac{1}{12} \\ + \frac{1}{4} \\ \hline \end{array}$

17. $\begin{array}{r} 2\frac{1}{3} \\ + 3\frac{1}{2} \\ \hline \end{array}$

18. $\begin{array}{r} 4\frac{5}{7} \\ + 2\frac{3}{14} \\ \hline \end{array}$

19. $\begin{array}{r} 7\frac{3}{4} \\ + 2\frac{1}{5} \\ \hline \end{array}$

20. $\begin{array}{r} 1\frac{2}{3} \\ + 2\frac{1}{4} \\ \hline \end{array}$

21. $\begin{array}{r} 2\frac{5}{8} \\ + 1\frac{5}{6} \\ \hline \end{array}$

22. $\begin{array}{r} 3\frac{4}{5} \\ + 2\frac{2}{3} \\ \hline \end{array}$

23. $\begin{array}{r} 4\frac{3}{10} \\ + 3\frac{13}{20} \\ \hline \end{array}$

24. $\begin{array}{r} 8\frac{11}{12} \\ + 3\frac{1}{4} \\ \hline \end{array}$

CHAPTER 30

Subtracting Fractions with Unlike Denominators

Bailey buys $\frac{11}{12}$ yd of wrapping paper. She uses $\frac{1}{3}$ yd to wrap a gift. How much wrapping paper does she have left?

To find out, subtract.

Step 1   **Step 2**   **Step 3**

$$\frac{11}{12}$$ $$\frac{11}{12} = \frac{11}{12}$$ $$\frac{11}{12} = \frac{11}{12}$$

$$-\frac{1}{3}$$ $$-\frac{1}{3} = \frac{4}{12}$$ $$-\frac{1}{3} = \frac{4}{12}$$

$$\frac{7}{12}$$

> Write the difference in simplest form.

Step 1   Determine if the denominators are the same.

Step 2   Change $\frac{1}{3}$ to an equivalent fraction with a common denominator.

Step 3   Subtract. Write the difference in simplest form.

Bailey has $\frac{7}{12}$ yd of paper left.

Example: Subtract: $\frac{6}{8} - \frac{1}{4}$.

Step 1   **Step 2**   **Step 3**

$$\frac{6}{8}$$ $$\frac{6}{8} = \frac{6}{8}$$ $$\frac{6}{8} = \frac{6}{8}$$

$$-\frac{1}{4}$$ $$-\frac{1}{4} = \frac{2}{8}$$ $$-\frac{1}{4} = \frac{2}{8}$$

$$\frac{4}{8} = \frac{1}{2}$$

> Write the difference in simplest form.

Remember, you can only subtract fractions with like denominators.

Example: Subtract $1\frac{1}{6}$ from $3\frac{2}{3}$.

Step 1 $\qquad$ Step 2 $\qquad$ Step 3

$$3\frac{2}{3} = 3\frac{4}{6}$$
$$-1\frac{1}{6} = 1\frac{1}{6}$$

$$3\frac{2}{3} = 3\frac{4}{6}$$
$$-1\frac{1}{6} = 1\frac{1}{6}$$
$$\frac{3}{6}$$

$$3\frac{2}{3} = 3\frac{4}{6}$$
$$-1\frac{1}{6} = 1\frac{1}{6}$$
$$2\frac{3}{6} = 2\frac{1}{2}$$

> Write the difference in simplest form.

Step 1 $\quad$ Write equivalent fractions with a common denominator.

Step 2 $\quad$ Subtract the fractions.

Step 3 $\quad$ Subtract the whole numbers.

Example: Pat bought $4\frac{3}{4}$ yd of fabric. She used $2\frac{3}{5}$ yd to make a costume for her son. How much fabric is left?

To find out, subtract.

Step 1 $\qquad$ Step 2 $\qquad$ Step 3

$$4\frac{3}{4} = 4\frac{15}{20}$$
$$-2\frac{3}{5} = 2\frac{12}{20}$$

$$4\frac{3}{4} = 4\frac{15}{20}$$
$$-2\frac{3}{5} = 2\frac{12}{20}$$
$$\frac{3}{20}$$

$$4\frac{3}{4} = 4\frac{15}{20}$$
$$-2\frac{3}{5} = 2\frac{12}{20}$$
$$2\frac{3}{20}$$

> Write the difference in simplest form.

Step 1 $\quad$ Write equivalent fractions with a common denominator.

Step 2 $\quad$ Subtract the fractions.

Step 3 $\quad$ Subtract the whole numbers.

Exercise 30-A

Subtract.

1. $\dfrac{7}{8}$ $-\dfrac{1}{16}$

2. $\dfrac{2}{3}$ $-\dfrac{3}{9}$

3. $\dfrac{3}{4}$ $-\dfrac{1}{8}$

4. $\dfrac{3}{5}$ $-\dfrac{1}{10}$

5. $\dfrac{3}{4}$ $-\dfrac{1}{2}$

6. $\dfrac{1}{2}$ $-\dfrac{1}{6}$

7. $\dfrac{5}{8}$ $-\dfrac{1}{2}$

8. $\dfrac{4}{5}$ $-\dfrac{1}{2}$

9. $2\dfrac{1}{2}$ $-1\dfrac{2}{7}$

10. $4\dfrac{1}{2}$ $-2\dfrac{1}{3}$

11. $5\dfrac{1}{4}$ $-2\dfrac{1}{12}$

12. $6\dfrac{7}{9}$ $-2\dfrac{1}{3}$

13. $5\dfrac{1}{3}$ $-2\dfrac{1}{4}$

14. $3\dfrac{2}{3}$ $-1\dfrac{1}{2}$

15. $6\dfrac{3}{5}$ $-2\dfrac{1}{10}$

16. $8\dfrac{5}{6}$ $-3\dfrac{1}{8}$

Exercise 30-B

Solve.

17. Dorothy has $3\dfrac{3}{4}$ h to spend in the computer lab. She spent $1\dfrac{1}{2}$ h learning a new program. How much time does she have left to spend in the lab? _____

18. Valerie needs $\dfrac{5}{8}$ yd of lace. She has $\dfrac{1}{3}$ yd. How much more lace does she need? _____

CHAPTER 31

Problem Solving Strategy: Using a Circle Graph

Sylvia asked 12 friends what type of books they liked to read. She uses the results of her survey to make a **circle graph**.

Type of Book	Number of People	Fraction
Mystery	3	$\frac{3}{12} = \frac{1}{4}$
Romance	5	$\frac{5}{12}$
Biography	2	$\frac{2}{12} = \frac{1}{6}$
Adventure	1	$\frac{1}{12}$
Science Fiction	1	$\frac{1}{12}$
Total	12	$\frac{12}{12} = 1$

Sylvia divides the circle in 12 equal parts because the fractions are in twelfths. Then she labels the graph with the information from the table above.

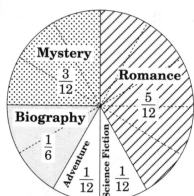

Which fraction shows biography as the favorite type of book? $\frac{1}{6}$

What fraction shows romance as the favorite type of book? $\frac{5}{12}$

Do more people like adventure books than mystery books?

Which is less, the fraction of people who chose science fiction or biography books?

Exercise 31-A

Use the circle graph at the right to answer these questions.

Favorite Kind of Music

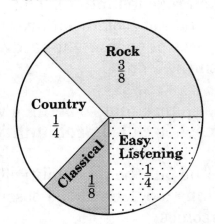

1. What fraction of the people like rock music the best?

   _____

2. Do more people like country or classical music the best?

   _____

3. What fraction of the people like easy listening music?

   _____

4. What is the difference between the fraction of people who like rock music and country music?

   _____

5. Which kind of music do the fewest people like? _____

6. Which is greater, the fraction of people who like rock music or the sum of the people who like country music and easy listening?

   _____

Exercise 31-B

Write the fraction for each part of the circle graph.

Bowling _____   Football _____

Soccer _____   Baseball _____

APPLICATION

Probability

If you reached into the bag and did not look, what are the chances of picking the card with the 5 on it?

The chance that something will happen is called **probability**.

To find out the probability of picking a 5, look at the possible outcomes.

There are 7 number cards altogether. One of the cards is a 5. Therefore, your chances of picking the 5 are 1 out of 7.

You can represent the probability as a fraction:

$$\frac{\text{number of 5 cards}}{\text{total number of cards}}$$

The probability of picking a 5 is $\frac{1}{7}$.

Complete.

1. What is the probability of drawing a 4? _____

2. What is the probability of drawing a 6? _____

3. What is the probability of drawing a 7? _____

4. What is the probability of drawing a 1? _____

5. There is _____ chance in _____ of drawing a 2.

6. There are _____ chances in _____ of drawing a 1.

7. There are _____ chances in _____ of drawing a 9.

Quiz for **UNIT 4**

Write the fraction.

1. three fifths _____   **2.** one third _____   **3.** six sevenths _____

Write the equivalent fraction.

4. $\dfrac{1}{3} = \dfrac{\Box}{9}$ **5.** $\dfrac{2}{5} = \dfrac{4}{\Box}$ **6.** $\dfrac{8}{9} = \dfrac{16}{\Box}$ **7.** $\dfrac{4}{7} = \dfrac{\Box}{14}$

Write the fraction in simplest form.

8. $\dfrac{8}{24} = \dfrac{\Box}{3}$ **9.** $\dfrac{5}{15} = \dfrac{1}{\Box}$ **10.** $\dfrac{6}{12} = \dfrac{\Box}{2}$ **11.** $\dfrac{4}{20} = \dfrac{1}{\Box}$

Add. Write the sum in simplest form.

12. $\dfrac{2}{4} + \dfrac{1}{4} =$ _____   **13.** $\dfrac{1}{6} + \dfrac{4}{6} =$ _____   **14.** $\dfrac{7}{9} + \dfrac{1}{9} =$ _____

15. $\quad \dfrac{1}{3}$ **16.** $\quad \dfrac{2}{5}$ **17.** $\quad 5\dfrac{1}{6}$ **18.** $\quad 4\dfrac{6}{7}$

$+ \ \dfrac{2}{6}$ $+ \ \dfrac{3}{10}$ $+ \ 2\dfrac{3}{18}$ $+ \ 4\dfrac{3}{14}$

Subtract.

19. $\quad \dfrac{8}{9}$ **20.** $\quad \dfrac{1}{4}$ **21.** $\quad 3\dfrac{1}{2}$ **22.** $\quad 5\dfrac{3}{4}$

$- \ \dfrac{4}{9}$ $- \ \dfrac{1}{12}$ $- \ 1\dfrac{1}{8}$ $- \ 2\dfrac{1}{24}$

CUMULATIVE REVIEW

Circle the letter of the correct answer.

Multiply.

1. 3.82 x 1.45
   a. 5.0539
   b. 5.539
   c. 5.439
   d. none of these

2. 0.073 x 0.4
   a. 0.292
   b. 0.2902
   c. 0.0292
   d. none of these

Divide.

3. 0.4 ÷ 3.89
   a. 9.725
   b. 97.25
   c. 0.9725
   d. none of these

Complete.

4. 120 s = __?__ min
   a. 7,200
   b. 3
   c. 2
   d. none of these

5. __?__ ft = 108 in.
   a. 80
   b. 8
   c. 9
   d. none of these

6. __?__ qt = 1 gal
   a. 4
   b. 6
   c. 8
   d. none of these

7. $\frac{6}{18} = \frac{\square}{3}$

   a. 1
   b. 2
   c. 6
   d. none of these

8. Write $\frac{7}{49}$ in simplest form.

   a. $\frac{1}{7}$
   b. $\frac{7}{7}$
   c. 1
   d. none of these

Add.

9. $\frac{1}{4} + \frac{2}{4}$

   a. $\frac{3}{4}$
   b. $\frac{1}{4}$
   c. $\frac{3}{8}$
   d. none of these

10. $\frac{3}{8} + \frac{2}{5}$

    a. $\frac{5}{13}$
    b. $\frac{31}{40}$
    c. $\frac{5}{8}$
    d. none of these

11. $5\frac{5}{8} + 2\frac{1}{3}$

    a. $8\frac{1}{3}$
    b. $7\frac{23}{24}$
    c. $7\frac{3}{24}$
    d. none of these

Subtract.

12. $\frac{7}{10} - \frac{1}{10}$

    a. $\frac{4}{5}$
    b. $\frac{6}{10}$
    c. $\frac{8}{10}$
    d. none of these

13. $\frac{2}{5} - \frac{1}{10}$

    a. $\frac{3}{10}$
    b. $\frac{1}{5}$
    c. $\frac{2}{5}$
    d. none of these

14. $8\frac{7}{9} - 3\frac{5}{18}$

    a. $5\frac{1}{3}$
    b. $5\frac{2}{9}$
    c. $5\frac{1}{2}$
    d. none of these

Multiplying and Dividing Fractions

There are 24 people in Bill's department. One third of them use computers. How many people in Bill's department use computers?

CHAPTER 32

Multiplying Fractions and Whole Numbers

Mrs. Chandler supervises 18 cashiers in her department. Two thirds of them work at night. How many cashiers work at night?

Think: The word *of* implies multiplication. It means *part of a whole*.

$$18 \times \frac{2}{3} = \frac{18 \times 2}{3} = \frac{36}{3} = 12$$

Step 1   Multiply the numerator by the whole number.

Step 2   Write the product over the denominator.

Step 3   Write the fraction in simplest form.

Example: What is $\frac{1}{8}$ of 12?

$$12 \times \frac{1}{8} = \frac{12 \times 1}{8} = \frac{12}{8} = 1\frac{4}{8} = 1\frac{1}{2}$$

Changing the order of the factors does not change the product.

$$\frac{1}{8} \times 12 = \frac{1 \times 12}{8} = \frac{12}{8} = 1\frac{4}{8} = 1\frac{2}{4} = 1\frac{1}{2}$$

CALCULATING

You can use a calculator to multiply a fraction and a whole number.

Multiply $4 \times \frac{3}{8}$.

Press: 4 ☒ 3 ÷ 8 ═ 1.5

Check: $4 \times \frac{3}{8} = \frac{4 \times 3}{8} = \frac{12}{8} = 1\frac{1}{2}$

Think: Are $1\frac{1}{2}$ and 1.5 equal?

Exercise 32-A

Multiply. Write the product in simplest form.

1. $3 \times \frac{1}{4}$ _____

2. $4 \times \frac{4}{5}$ _____

3. $\frac{1}{3} \times 7$ _____

4. $\frac{2}{5} \times 3$ _____

5. $20 \times \frac{3}{7}$ _____

6. $14 \times \frac{3}{4}$ _____

7. $\frac{2}{3} \times 10$ _____

8. $\frac{5}{12} \times 6$ _____

9. $5 \times \frac{3}{4}$ _____

10. $\frac{2}{9} \times 4$ _____

11. $\frac{1}{8} \times 8$ _____

12. $\frac{6}{7} \times 11$ _____

13. $9 \times \frac{1}{4}$ _____

14. $33 \times \frac{1}{6}$ _____

15. $\frac{1}{11} \times 6$ _____

16. $9 \times \frac{3}{10}$ _____

Exercise 32-B

Solve.

17. There are 16 customers in line at the bank. One fourth of them are making deposits only. How many people are making deposits? _____

18. It is $\frac{7}{10}$ of a mile from Rebecca's office to the bus stop. How far does Rebecca walk to and from the bus stop each day? _____

19. There are 24 people in Joe's computer class. Two thirds of them were in his class last semester. How many people were in his class last semester? _____

Multiplying Fractions

Multiply $\frac{1}{2}$ x $\frac{1}{4}$,

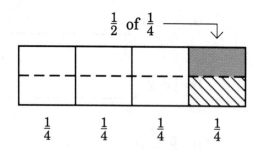

$\frac{1}{2}$ of $\frac{1}{4}$

$\frac{1}{4}$ $\frac{1}{4}$ $\frac{1}{4}$ $\frac{1}{4}$

$$\frac{1}{2} \times \frac{1}{4} = \frac{1 \times 1}{2 \times 4} = \frac{1}{8}$$

> To multiply two fractions, first multiply the numerators. Then multiply the denominators.

$$\frac{1}{8} < \frac{1}{4} \qquad \frac{1}{8} < \frac{1}{2}$$

> Since you are multiplying two amounts less than 1, the product will be less than either fraction.

Example: It took Suzanne $\frac{2}{3}$ hour to mow the lawn last week. It took her $\frac{3}{4}$ as long this week. What fraction of an hour did it take Suzanne to mow the lawn this week?

To find out, multiply $\frac{2}{3}$ and $\frac{3}{4}$.

$$\frac{3}{4} \times \frac{2}{3} = \frac{3 \times 2}{4 \times 3} = \frac{6}{12} = \frac{1}{2}$$

Step 1   Multiply the numerators.

Step 2   Multiply the denominators.

Step 3   Write the product in simplest form.

It took Suzanne $\frac{1}{2}$ hour to mow the lawn this week.

Multiply. Write the product in simplest form.

1. $\frac{1}{3} \times \frac{1}{2}$ _____

2. $\frac{1}{4} \times \frac{1}{5}$ _____

3. $\frac{1}{6} \times \frac{1}{7}$ _____

4. $\frac{5}{8} \times \frac{1}{3}$ _____

5. $\frac{6}{7} \times \frac{1}{4}$ _____

6. $\frac{5}{6} \times \frac{7}{10}$ _____

7. $\frac{1}{6} \times \frac{3}{10}$ _____

8. $\frac{4}{5} \times \frac{1}{3}$ _____

9. $\frac{2}{9} \times \frac{5}{6}$ _____

10. $\frac{11}{12} \times \frac{1}{10}$ _____

11. $\frac{1}{12} \times \frac{2}{15}$ _____

12. $\frac{2}{3} \times \frac{5}{12}$ _____

13. $\frac{7}{9} \times \frac{1}{3}$ _____

14. $\frac{1}{3} \times \frac{3}{5}$ _____

15. $\frac{1}{4} \times \frac{1}{6}$ _____

16. $\frac{1}{2} \times \frac{1}{16}$ _____

17. $\frac{7}{10} \times \frac{2}{5}$ _____

18. $\frac{2}{5} \times \frac{3}{5}$ _____

Exercise 33-B

Owen is making Blue Cheese Dip. He makes only half of the recipe. Use the information at the right to answer each question.

19. How much of each ingredient should Owen use?

_____

_____

_____

_____

_____

Blue Cheese Dip
$\frac{1}{2}$ c crumbled blue cheese
$\frac{3}{4}$ c yogurt
$\frac{1}{3}$ tsp lemon juice
$\frac{1}{4}$ c sour cream
$\frac{1}{8}$ tsp garlic powder
Mix all the ingredients together. Chill.

20. Owen used only $\frac{1}{3}$ of the dip he made.

What fraction of the recipe did he use? _____

CHAPTER 34

Multiplying Mixed Numbers

Helene is buying carpeting for the family room.
The room measures $7\frac{1}{2}$ ft wide and $8\frac{1}{3}$ ft long.
How much carpeting is needed to cover the floor?

To find out, multiply, $7\frac{1}{2}$ x $8\frac{1}{3}$.

Step 1   Write the mixed numbers as fractions by multiplying the denominator by the whole number. Add the numerator. Write this number over the denominator.

$$\boxed{2 \times 7 + 1}\!\!\!> \quad 7\frac{1}{2} = \frac{15}{2} \qquad \boxed{3 \times 8 + 1}\!\!\!> \quad 8\frac{1}{3} = \frac{25}{3}$$

Step 2   Multiply the numerators. Multiply the denominators.

$$\frac{15}{2} \times \frac{25}{3} = \frac{15 \times 25}{2 \times 3} = \frac{375}{6} = 62\frac{1}{2} \quad \boxed{\text{Write the product in simplest form.}}$$

Helene needs $62\frac{1}{2}$ square feet of carpeting.

Example: Luke worked at the community center for $3\frac{1}{4}$ h each day for 4 days. How many hours did he work?

$$3\frac{1}{4} \times 4$$

$$\frac{13}{4} \times 4 \quad \boxed{\text{Write the mixed number as a fraction.}}$$

$$\frac{13}{4} \times 4 = \frac{13 \times 4}{4} = \frac{52}{4} = 13 \quad \boxed{\text{Write the product in simplest form.}}$$

Luke worked 13 hours.

Exercise 34-A

Multiply. Write the product in simplest form.

1. $2\frac{1}{2}$ x $\frac{1}{3}$ _____

2. $3\frac{1}{4}$ x $\frac{2}{5}$ _____

3. $\frac{1}{3}$ x $1\frac{3}{4}$ _____

4. $\frac{3}{4}$ x $1\frac{1}{10}$ _____

5. $2\frac{3}{8}$ x $1\frac{1}{2}$ _____

6. $4\frac{4}{5}$ x $2\frac{3}{10}$ _____

7. $3\frac{6}{7}$ x $4\frac{2}{3}$ _____

8. $5\frac{1}{6}$ x 3 _____

9. $6\frac{1}{2}$ x 3 _____

10. $2\frac{3}{5}$ x 7 _____

11. 9 x $1\frac{1}{3}$ _____

12. $2\frac{1}{9}$ x 0 _____

13. $8\frac{1}{3}$ x $\frac{4}{5}$ _____

14. 5 x $3\frac{1}{5}$ _____

15. $10\frac{1}{2}$ x $3\frac{4}{7}$ _____

16. $3\frac{12}{13}$ x 1 _____

17. $4\frac{1}{6}$ x $\frac{2}{3}$ _____

18. $\frac{1}{4}$ x $3\frac{5}{6}$ _____

19. $1\frac{8}{9}$ x 3 _____

20. $\frac{8}{11}$ x $3\frac{1}{10}$ _____

21. 9 x $1\frac{2}{9}$ _____

Exercise 34-B

Solve.

22. Jackie is wallpapering 3 rooms in her house. It takes her $6\frac{1}{2}$ h to finish one room. How long will it take her to finish 3 rooms? _____

23. Wanda's Wallcoverings is open $8\frac{2}{3}$ h each day. Benny works $\frac{3}{4}$ of the time the store is open. How many hours does he work? _____

24. Wanda bought $3\frac{1}{4}$ yd of decorative ribbon. She used $2\frac{2}{3}$ yd. How much ribbon does she have left over? _____

CHAPTER 35

Dividing a Whole Number by a Fraction

Carrie is serving shrimp cocktail to her guests. She uses $\frac{1}{2}$ lemon for each plate. If she has 4 lemons, how many guests can she serve?

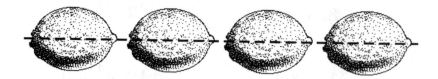

There are 8 halves in 4 lemons.

$$4 \div \frac{1}{2} = 8$$

Carrie can serve 8 guests.

Dividing a number gives the same result as multiplying by the *reciprocal* of the number. Two numbers whose product is 1 are **reciprocals**.

$$2 \times \frac{1}{2} = 1, \text{ so } 2 \text{ and } \frac{1}{2} \text{ are reciprocals.}$$

Instead of dividing by $\frac{1}{2}$ you can multiply by 2.

$$4 \div \frac{1}{2} = 8 \qquad 4 \times 2 = 8$$

Example: How many $\frac{1}{3}$s are in 4?

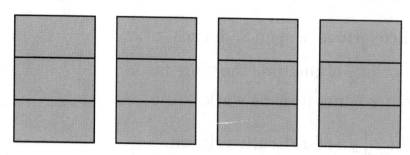

$$4 \div \frac{1}{3} = 3 \times 4 = 12$$

Exercise 35-A

What is the reciprocal of each number?

1. $\frac{1}{2}$ _____   2. $\frac{1}{4}$ _____   3. $\frac{6}{7}$ _____   4. $\frac{4}{9}$ _____

Exercise 35-B

5. How many $\frac{1}{2}$s in 3?

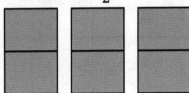

6. How many $\frac{1}{3}$s in 3?

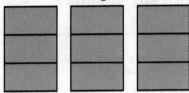

_____   _____

Exercise 35-C

Divide. Write the quotient in simplest form.

7. $1 \div \frac{1}{5}$ _____   8. $6 \div \frac{1}{3}$ _____   9. $4 \div \frac{1}{4}$ _____

10. $8 \div \frac{3}{10}$ _____   11. $2 \div \frac{1}{8}$ _____   12. $5 \div \frac{1}{6}$ _____

13. $3 \div \frac{1}{4}$ _____   14. $5 \div \frac{1}{5}$ _____   15. $6 \div \frac{1}{7}$ _____

16. $4 \div \frac{2}{5}$ _____   17. $8 \div \frac{4}{5}$ _____   18. $10 \div \frac{1}{5}$ _____

CRITICAL THINKING

19. When you divide a whole number by a fraction, will the quotient be greater than or less than the whole number? Explain your answer.

_____

_____

CHAPTER 36

Dividing a Fraction by a Whole Number

Doug used $\frac{1}{3}$ of a roll of wrapping paper to wrap 2 presents. How much paper did he use for each gift?

To find out, divide $\frac{1}{3}$ by 2.

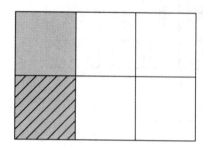

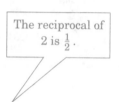

The reciprocal of 2 is $\frac{1}{2}$.

$$\frac{1}{3} \div 2 = \frac{1}{3} \times \frac{1}{2} = \frac{1}{6}$$

Step 1   Write the reciprocal of the whole number divisor.

Step 2   Multiply.

Example: Marcy has $\frac{2}{3}$ of a melon left over. She shares it equally among her 4 children. How much of the melon does each child receive?

To find out, divide $\frac{2}{3}$ by 4.

The reciprocal of 4 is $\frac{1}{4}$.

$$\frac{2}{3} \div 4 = \frac{2}{3} \times \frac{1}{4} = \frac{2}{12} = \frac{1}{6}$$

Step 1   Write the reciprocal of 4.

Step 2   Multiply.

Step 3   Write the quotient in simplest form.

CT
CRITICAL THINKING   When you divide a fraction by a whole number, will the quotient be greater than or less than the dividend?

Exercise 36-A

What is the reciprocal of each number?

1. 3 _____   **2.** 5 _____   **3.** 7 _____   **4.** 19 _____

Exercise 36-B

Divide. Write the quotient in simplest form.

5. $\frac{1}{3} \div 3$ _____   **6.** $\frac{2}{5} \div 4$ _____   **7.** $\frac{3}{8} \div 5$ _____

8. $\frac{2}{3} \div 5$ _____   **9.** $\frac{1}{6} \div 9$ _____   **10.** $\frac{6}{7} \div 4$ _____

11. $\frac{3}{11} \div 10$ _____   **12.** $\frac{1}{9} \div 7$ _____   **13.** $\frac{1}{4} \div 4$ _____

14. $\frac{1}{8} \div 4$ _____   **15.** $\frac{2}{7} \div 4$ _____   **16.** $\frac{2}{5} \div 5$ _____

17. $\frac{1}{6} \div 6$ _____   **18.** $\frac{5}{6} \div 5$ _____   **19.** $\frac{2}{3} \div 3$ _____

20. $\frac{1}{4} \div 3$ _____   **21.** $\frac{3}{4} \div 4$ _____   **22.** $\frac{2}{5} \div 7$ _____

Exercise 36-C

Complete.

23.

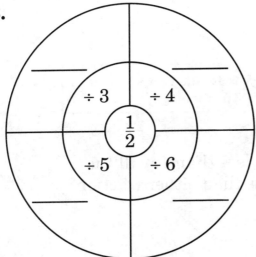

24.

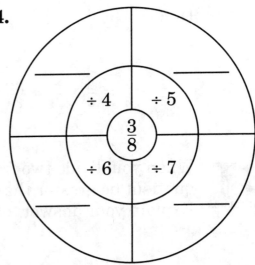

CHAPTER 37

Dividing a Fraction by a Fraction

Paula has $\frac{3}{4}$ yd of ribbon. She cuts it into pieces that measure $\frac{1}{8}$ yd long. How many pieces does she have now?

To find out, divide.

$$\frac{3}{4} \div \frac{1}{8} = \frac{3}{4} \times \frac{8}{1} = \frac{24}{4} = 6$$

Step 1   Write the reciprocal of the divisor. To write the reciprocal of a fraction, reverse the numerator and the denominator.

Step 2   Multiply.

Step 3   Write the quotient in simplest form.

Paula has 6 pieces of ribbon.

Example: Rick is developing film in the darkroom. Each roll of film needs $\frac{1}{6}$ bottle of developer. If he has a bottle of developer that is $\frac{2}{3}$ full, how many rolls of film can he develop?

Divide $\frac{2}{3}$ by $\frac{1}{6}$.

$$\frac{2}{3} \div \frac{1}{6} = \frac{2}{3} \times \frac{6}{1} = \frac{12}{3} = 4$$

Write the reciprocal of $\frac{1}{6}$. Then multiply.

CT
CRITICAL THINKING   When you divide two fractions less than 1, will the quotient be greater than or less than either fraction? Explain your answer.

Exercise 37-A

What is the reciprocal of each number?

1. $\frac{4}{5}$ _____

2. $\frac{3}{4}$ _____

3. $\frac{2}{3}$ _____

4. $\frac{8}{7}$ _____

Exercise 37-B

Divide. Write the quotient in simplest form.

5. $\frac{5}{6} \div \frac{4}{9}$ _____

6. $\frac{4}{5} \div \frac{1}{5}$ _____

7. $\frac{10}{9} \div \frac{4}{3}$ _____

8. $\frac{3}{5} \div \frac{2}{3}$ _____

9. $\frac{3}{8} \div \frac{3}{4}$ _____

10. $\frac{4}{5} \div \frac{1}{10}$ _____

11. $\frac{7}{10} \div \frac{1}{6}$ _____

12. $\frac{5}{8} \div \frac{1}{4}$ _____

13. $\frac{2}{9} \div \frac{4}{3}$ _____

14. $\frac{2}{5} \div \frac{5}{8}$ _____

15. $\frac{1}{4} \div \frac{1}{3}$ _____

16. $\frac{2}{3} \div \frac{2}{9}$ _____

17. $\frac{1}{2} \div \frac{7}{16}$ _____

18. $\frac{1}{3} \div \frac{3}{4}$ _____

19. $\frac{5}{6} \div \frac{7}{12}$ _____

20. $\frac{3}{8} \div \frac{3}{8}$ _____

21. $\frac{1}{2} \div \frac{2}{3}$ _____

22. $\frac{3}{4} \div \frac{3}{8}$ _____

WRITING IN MATH

Explain in your own words the relationship between multiplication and division of fractions. Why do you multiply when dividing fractions? How can the quotient be greater than both the dividend and the divisor? Give examples.

_____

_____

_____

CHAPTER 38

Dividing with Mixed Numbers

David can design a company logo in $8\frac{1}{2}$ h. He works on the logo for $2\frac{1}{8}$ h each day. If he continues at this pace, how many days should it take him to complete the logo?

$$8\frac{1}{2} \div 2\frac{1}{8} = \frac{17}{2} \div \frac{17}{8}$$

$$= \frac{17}{2} \times \frac{8}{17} \qquad \text{The reciprocal of } \frac{17}{8} \text{ is } \frac{8}{17}.$$

$$= \frac{136}{34} = 4$$

Step 1   Write the mixed numbers as fractions.

Step 2   Write the reciprocal of the divisor.

Step 3   Multiply.

David will need 4 days to complete the logo.

Example: Divide: $9\frac{2}{5} \div \frac{1}{2}$

$$\boxed{5 \times 9 + 2} \rightarrow 9\frac{2}{5} = \frac{47}{5} \div \frac{1}{2}$$

$$= \frac{47}{5} \times \frac{2}{1} \qquad \text{The reciprocal of } \frac{1}{2} \text{ is 2. Multiply.}$$

$$= \frac{95}{5} = 18\frac{4}{5} \qquad \text{Write the quotient in simplest form.}$$

When you divide two mixed numbers, will the quotient be greater than or less than either mixed number? Explain.

When you divide a mixed number by a fraction, will the quotient be greater than or less than the mixed number? Explain.

Exercise 38-A

Write the mixed number as a fraction. Then write the reciprocal of the fraction.

1. $3\frac{1}{2}$ _____

2. $4\frac{4}{5}$ _____

3. $6\frac{2}{3}$ _____

4. $1\frac{3}{8}$ _____

5. $2\frac{1}{12}$ _____

6. $8\frac{1}{7}$ _____

Exercise 38-B

Divide. Write the quotient in simplest form.

7. $3 \div 5\frac{1}{3}$ _____

8. $6 \div 2\frac{3}{4}$ _____

9. $4 \div 1\frac{1}{2}$ _____

10. $3\frac{1}{2} \div \frac{7}{10}$ _____

11. $1\frac{3}{4} \div \frac{1}{2}$ _____

12. $2\frac{2}{5} \div 4$ _____

13. $3\frac{3}{4} \div 3$ _____

14. $1\frac{1}{3} \div 12$ _____

15. $5\frac{1}{4} \div 9$ _____

16. $3\frac{3}{4} \div 2\frac{1}{2}$ _____

17. $8\frac{1}{3} \div 3\frac{1}{3}$ _____

18. $1\frac{3}{20} \div 1\frac{4}{5}$ _____

19. $20 \div 2\frac{2}{3}$ _____

20. $3\frac{5}{9} \div 4\frac{4}{9}$ _____

21. $6\frac{1}{2} \div 9\frac{3}{4}$ _____

22. $14 \div 5\frac{1}{4}$ _____

23. $7 \div 3\frac{1}{9}$ _____

24. $\frac{4}{5} \div 1\frac{5}{7}$ _____

CRITICAL THINKING

Use the numbers in the triangle to make the greatest possible quotient and the least possible quotient.

25.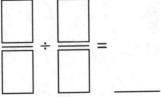

26.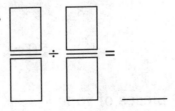

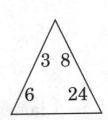

CHAPTER 39

Problem Solving Strategy: Choose the Correct Operation

Before you solve a problem, you need to make a plan. The plan tells which operation to use.

When the words in the problem suggest:

1) joining or finding a total, add.
2) finding how much greater one group is than another, subtract.
3) joining sets with the same number, multiply.
4) finding how many are in each group, divide.

Example: Betty worked 12 hours on Saturday. Maura worked $\frac{3}{4}$ of the time Betty worked. How many hours did Maura work?

The words *of the time* suggest multiplication.

$$12 \times \frac{3}{4} = \frac{12}{1} \times \frac{3}{4} = \frac{36}{4} = 9$$

Maura worked 9 hours.

Example: James has $3\frac{1}{3}$ yd of rope. He cut it into pieces $\frac{1}{6}$ yd long. How many pieces of rope does he have?

$$3\frac{1}{3} \div \frac{1}{6} = \frac{10}{3} \div \frac{1}{6}$$

$$= \frac{10}{3} \times \frac{6}{1}$$

$$= \frac{60}{3} = 20$$

James has 20 pieces of rope.

Tell which operation you used to solve each problem.
Then solve.

1. Maria worked $6\frac{1}{2}$ hours on Monday. Neil worked $1\frac{1}{2}$ times as long. How many hours did Neil work? _____

2. Rachel rode her exercise bicycle $8\frac{1}{2}$ hours last week and 3 hours this week. How many hours did she ride during these two weeks? _____

3. Sandy's Gravel Company loaded $\frac{3}{8}$ T of gravel onto 2 trucks. What amount of gravel was loaded onto each truck? _____

4. Mr. Ramirez bought a roll of wire $\frac{5}{6}$ yd long. He cut it into pieces $\frac{1}{12}$ yd long. How many pieces of wire does he have now? _____

5. Mel put $\frac{1}{3}$ of his paycheck into his savings account. He used $\frac{1}{4}$ of his check to pay his rent. What fraction of his paycheck does he have left? _____

6. Robin had $\frac{2}{3}$ lb of potato salad left over from a cookout. She shared it equally among her 3 children. How much did each child receive? _____

7. Barbara worked $32\frac{1}{2}$ h last week and 40 h this week. How many more hours did she work this week than last week? _____

APPLICATION

Recipes

Fractions are used in cooking to indicate how much of each ingredient is needed for a given recipe. You may want to adjust the measures to make a larger or smaller quantity than the recipe calls for.

Solve.

1. David uses this recipe for molasses bread. He needs to make 1 loaf. How much of each ingredient does he need?

   _____

   _____

   _____

   _____

   _____

   Molasses Bread

2 eggs	3 tsp baking powder
2 c bran	$1\frac{1}{4}$ tsp baking soda
2 c flour	$\frac{1}{2}$ c molasses
$\frac{1}{2}$ c sugar	2 c buttermilk
$\frac{1}{2}$ tsp salt	$\frac{1}{2}$ c oil

   Makes 2 loaves.

2. Molly is making blueberry muffins. She needs $1\frac{1}{2}$ dozen muffins. How much of each ingredient does she need?

   _____

   _____

   _____

   _____

   Blueberry Muffins

$\frac{3}{4}$ c flour	1 c whole wheat flour
$\frac{1}{4}$ c sugar	1 c blueberries
$\frac{3}{4}$ tsp salt	$\frac{3}{4}$ c buttermilk
2 eggs	1 tsp baking powder
$\frac{1}{3}$ c salad oil	$\frac{1}{4}$ tsp baking soda

   Makes 1 dozen muffins

 uiz for **UNIT 5**

Multiply. Write the product in simplest form.

1. $2 \times \frac{1}{2}$ _____

2. $4 \times \frac{1}{3}$ _____

3. $\frac{3}{5} \times 7$ _____

4. $8 \times \frac{2}{3}$ _____

5. $\frac{1}{2} \times \frac{3}{4}$ _____

6. $\frac{1}{8} \times \frac{4}{5}$ _____

7. $\frac{3}{4} \times \frac{4}{7}$ _____

8. $\frac{7}{10} \times \frac{2}{5}$ _____

9. $\frac{7}{8} \times \frac{1}{4}$ _____

10. $2\frac{5}{6} \times 5$ _____

11. $1 \times 3\frac{4}{5}$ _____

12. $3\frac{2}{5} \times 1\frac{1}{2}$ _____

13. $8\frac{1}{3} \times 7$ _____

14. $2\frac{1}{3} \times 3\frac{1}{9}$ _____

15. $\frac{6}{7} \times 4\frac{1}{8}$ _____

What is the reciprocal of each number?

16. $\frac{1}{3}$ ____

17. $\frac{4}{5}$ ____

18. $\frac{9}{10}$ ____

19. $\frac{11}{3}$ ____

20. 3 ____

21. 9 ____

22. 16 ____

23. 41 ____

Divide. Write the quotient in simplest form.

24. $1 \div \frac{1}{3}$ _____

25. $4 \div \frac{1}{5}$ _____

26. $6 \div \frac{1}{3}$ _____

27. $\frac{1}{4} \div 8$ _____

28. $\frac{3}{8} \div 21$ _____

29. $\frac{3}{4} \div 9$ _____

30. $\frac{1}{2} \div \frac{1}{2}$ _____

31. $\frac{3}{4} \div \frac{1}{3}$ _____

32. $\frac{3}{5} \div \frac{1}{4}$ _____

33. $\frac{2}{7} \div \frac{2}{3}$ _____

34. $4 \div 3\frac{1}{6}$ _____

35. $1\frac{4}{9} \div 8\frac{2}{3}$ _____

CUMULATIVE REVIEW

Circle the letter of the correct answer.

Complete.

1. 180 s = ____?____ min
   - a. 10,800
   - b. 3
   - c. 120
   - d. none of these

2. 24 ft = ____?____ in.
   - a. 2
   - b. 144
   - c. 288
   - d. none of these

3. 4 qt = ____?____ c
   - a. 8
   - b. 16
   - c. 2
   - d. none of these

Add or subtract. Write the answer in simplest form.

4. $\frac{1}{3} + \frac{2}{9}$
   - a. $\frac{5}{9}$
   - b. $\frac{2}{3}$
   - c. $\frac{3}{9}$
   - d. none of these

5. $2\frac{3}{8} + 4\frac{1}{6}$
   - a. $6\frac{13}{24}$
   - b. $6\frac{4}{24}$
   - c. 7
   - d. none of these

6. $8\frac{4}{7} - 2\frac{3}{14}$
   - a. $6\frac{1}{7}$
   - b. $6\frac{5}{14}$
   - c. 6
   - d. none of these

Multiply or divide. Write the answer in simplest form.

7. $2 \times \frac{1}{9}$
   - a. $\frac{1}{18}$
   - b. $2\frac{1}{9}$
   - c. $\frac{2}{9}$
   - d. none of these

8. $\frac{3}{4} \times \frac{2}{5}$
   - a. $\frac{5}{9}$
   - b. $\frac{5}{4}$
   - c. $\frac{3}{10}$
   - d. none of these

9. $2\frac{1}{5} \times 3\frac{3}{4}$
   - a. $8\frac{1}{4}$
   - b. $6\frac{3}{20}$
   - c. $8\frac{5}{20}$
   - d. none of these

10. $\frac{1}{9} \div 8$
    - a. 72
    - b. $\frac{72}{1}$
    - c. $\frac{1}{72}$
    - d. none of these

11. $\frac{3}{5} \div \frac{2}{9}$
    - a. $\frac{6}{45}$
    - b. $2\frac{7}{10}$
    - c. $\frac{27}{10}$
    - d. none of these

12. $3\frac{2}{9} \div 7\frac{1}{3}$
    - a. $7\frac{10}{29}$
    - b. $2\frac{1}{3}$
    - c. $\frac{29}{66}$
    - d. none of these

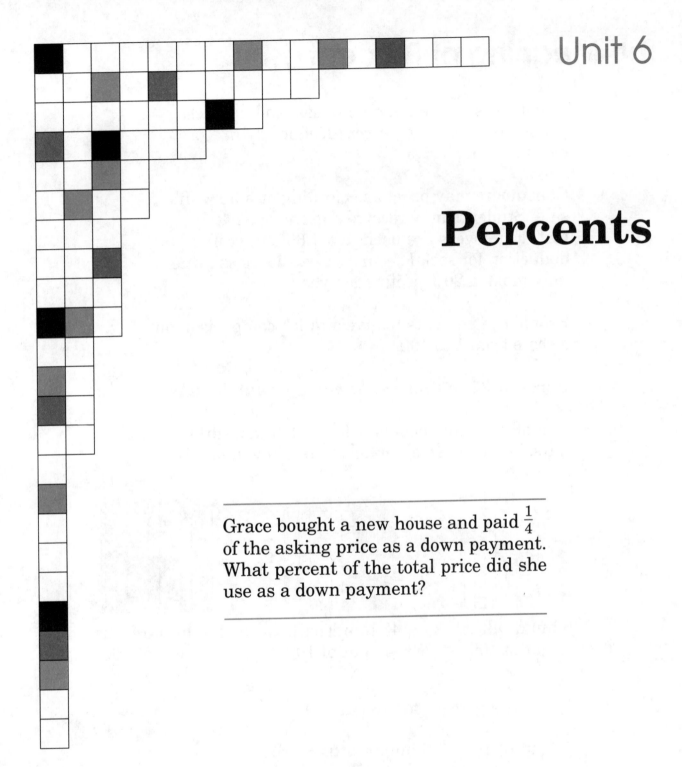

Percents

Grace bought a new house and paid $\frac{1}{4}$ of the asking price as a down payment. What percent of the total price did she use as a down payment?

CHAPTER 40

The Meaning of Percent

Consumers, students, employees, and business people use the word *percent* frequently in everyday life.

Consumers may purchase clothing at a 50% off sale. Students may receive a grade of 87% on a test. Employees are used to a 7.65% payroll deduction for social security tax. Business owners may make a 20% profit each year.

People use percents to give a quick comparison on a scale from 1 to 100.

Percent (%) means *per hundred* or *hundredths*.

The place value models below are hundredths flats. You can use a percent to tell how much is shaded.

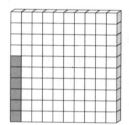

6 hundredths
6 out of 100
6%

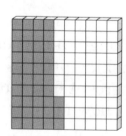

43 hundredths
43 out of 100
43%

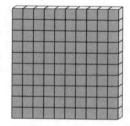

100 hundredths
100 out of 100
100%

Example: Write the percent for 16 out of 100.

16 out of 100 = 16 hundredths = 16%

Example: Write the percent for $7\frac{1}{2}$ hundredths.

$7\frac{1}{2}$ hundredths = $7\frac{1}{2}$ %

Exercise 40-A

What percent of each flat is shaded?

1.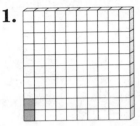

_____

2.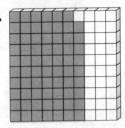

_____

3.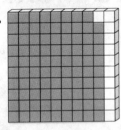

_____

Exercise 40-B

Write the percent.

4. 10 out of 100 _____

5. 13 out of 100 _____

6. 7 out of 100 _____

7. 0 out of 100 _____

8. 98 out of 100 _____

9. 67 out of 100 _____

10. 25 out of 100 _____

11. 18 out of 100 _____

Exercise 40-C

This chart shows the favorite months to take vacation of 100 employees. Use the chart to solve the problems.

12. How many employees said July was their favorite month to vacation?

_____

Favorite Vacation Months	
May	10
June	15
July	10
August	25
December	40

13. What percent of the employees named August as their favorite month to take a vacation? _____

14. What percent of the employees named either May or June as their favorite month to vacation?

_____

CHAPTER 41

Fractions and Percents

Fractions can be written as percents.

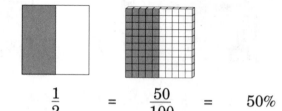

$$\frac{1}{2} \quad = \quad \frac{50}{100} \quad = \quad 50\%$$

When a fraction has a denominator of 100, just write the numerator with a percent symbol.

$$\frac{18}{100} = 18\% \qquad \frac{89}{100} = 89\%$$

Example: Write $\frac{7}{20}$ as a percent.

When a fraction has a denominator other than 100, write an equivalent fraction with a denominator of 100.

$$\frac{7}{20} = \frac{7 \times 5}{20 \times 5} = \frac{35}{100} = 35\%$$

> Write the numerator with a percent symbol.

You can also divide to write a fraction as a percent.

Example: Write $\frac{17}{25}$ as a percent.

$$\frac{17}{25} = 25\overline{)17.00}$$

$$\begin{array}{r} .68 \\ 25\overline{)17.00} \\ -15\,0 \\ \hline 2\,00 \\ -\,2\,00 \\ \hline 0 \end{array} = 68\%$$

Step 1   Divide the numerator by the denominator. Remember, adding zeros after the last digit of a decimal does not change its value.

Step 2   Rewrite 68 hundredths as a percent.

Exercise 41-A

Write as a percent.

1. $\dfrac{16}{100}$ _____

2. $\dfrac{81}{100}$ _____

3. $\dfrac{1}{100}$ _____

4. $\dfrac{3}{5}$ _____

5. $\dfrac{3}{4}$ _____

6. $\dfrac{16}{16}$ _____

7. $\dfrac{1}{2}$ _____

8. $\dfrac{9}{20}$ _____

9. $\dfrac{3}{10}$ _____

10. $\dfrac{113}{100}$ _____

11. $\dfrac{2}{5}$ _____

12. $\dfrac{6}{25}$ _____

Exercise 41-B

Write as a fraction.

13. 3% _____

14. 70% _____

15. 49% _____

16. 10% _____

17. 1% _____

18. 6% _____

19. 25% _____

20. 110% _____

21. 50% _____

22. 5% _____

23. 9% _____

24. 36% _____

25. 45% _____

26. 85% _____

27. 40% _____

CRITICAL THINKING

28. To what whole number is 100% equal? _____

29. Explain how you would determine if 24% is

greater than or less than $\dfrac{6}{25}$. _____

_____

CHAPTER 42

Decimals and Percents

Decimals can be written as percents.

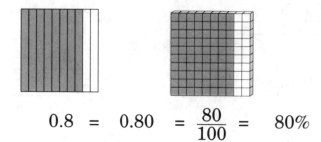

$$0.8 \;=\; 0.80 \;=\; \frac{80}{100} \;=\; 80\%$$

To write a decimal as a percent, express the decimal in hundredths.

Example: Write 0.5 as a percent.

        0.5 = 50 hundredths
        50 hundredths = 50%

Example: Write 0.827 as a percent.

        0.827   Move the decimal point two places to the right.

        0.827 = 82.7%

To change a percent to a decimal, write the number without the percent sign and move the decimal point two places to the *left*.

Example: Write 32% as a decimal.

        32% = 0.32   Move the decimal point two places to the left.

Exercise 42-A

Write as a percent.

1. 0.9 _____

2. 0.17 _____

3. 0.6 _____

4. 0.04 _____

5. 0.387 _____

6. 0.09_____

7. 0.517 _____

8. 0.23 _____

9. 0.5_____

10. 0.1 _____

11. 0.492 _____

12. 0.111 _____

13. 0.70 _____

14. 0.825 _____

15. 0.4 _____

Exercise 42-B

Write as a decimal.

16. 37% _____

17. 98% _____

18. 3% _____

19. 42.9% _____

20. 63.1% _____

21. 14.2% _____

22. 2.9% _____

23. 85% _____

24. 9% _____

25. 4.3% _____

26. 24% _____

27. 1% _____

28. 6.3% _____

29. 84.9% _____

30. 3.7% _____

CALCULATING

You can use a calculator to help you find percents.

$\frac{1}{3} \rightarrow$ 1 ÷ 3 = 0.3333333 → 0.333 = 33.3% ◁ **Round to thousandths.**

Write each fraction as a decimal and as a percent. Use a calculator.

31. $\frac{3}{8}$ _____

32. $\frac{7}{8}$ _____

33. $\frac{1}{6}$ _____

34. $\frac{1}{7}$ _____

CHAPTER 43

A Percent of a Number

A sweater that regularly sells for $48 is on sale for 20% off. How much will the savings be?

To find out a percent of a number, write the percent as a decimal and multiply.

Step 1   20% = 0.20

Step 2

$$
\begin{array}{r}
\$48 \\
\times\ 0.20 \\
\hline
00 \\
96 \\
\hline
\$9.60
\end{array}
$$

2 decimal places

The savings on the sweater is $9.60.

Example: Megan wants to spend 27% of her salary for child care. If she earns $2,500 per month, how much can she afford to spend on child care?

To find out, write the percent as a fraction and multiply.

Step 1 $\frac{27}{100}$ x $2500 = $\frac{67500}{100}$ = 675

Step 2   27% = $\frac{27}{100}$

She can afford to pay $675 per month.

CALCULATING

You can use the $\boxed{\%}$ key on a calculator to find a percent of a number.

Find: 30% of 80.

Press: 80 $\boxed{\text{x}}$ 30 $\boxed{\%}$ 24

Exercise 43-A

Use a fraction to find the number.

1. 20% of 62 _____

2. 16% of 95 _____

3. 6% of 49 _____

4. 43% of 80 _____

5. 20% of 140 _____

6. 35% of 55 _____

7. 49% of 110 _____

8. 64% of 85 _____

9. 90% of 180 _____

10. 91% of 150 _____

Exercise 43-B

Use a decimal to find the number.

11. 10% of 190 _____

12. 47% of 74 _____

13. 62% of 145 _____

14. 92% of 180 _____

15. 75% of 150 _____

16. 27% of 550 _____

17. 19% of 100 _____

18. 83% of 91 _____

19. 42% of 80 _____

20. 8% of 25 _____

CALCULATING

Use the % key on a calculator to find the following numbers. Round your answers to the nearest tenth or cent.

21. 12% of 55 _____

22. 19% of 80 _____

23. 14% of $38.70 _____

24. 20% of $229.99 _____

25. 80% of $120.00 _____

26. 15% of 90 _____

CHAPTER 44

Problem Solving: Using Percent

The local bookstore offers a certain percent off the cost of books to regular customers. The decrease in price is called the **discount**. What is the final cost of a $125 order with a 20% discount?

Step 1	Step 2	Step 3
20% = 0.20	$125 x 0.20 —————— 000 250 —————— $25.00	$125.00 – 25.00 —————— $100.00

Step 1   Write the percent as a decimal.

Step 2   Multiply the price of the books by the decimal.

Step 3   Subtract the discount from the original price.

The final cost is $100.00.

Example: Which is the better buy? A $30 video tape at a 25% discount or the same tape reduced by $10?

CALCULATING

Step 1   Find the discounted price of the $30 tape.

Press: 30 $\boxed{x}$ 25 $\boxed{\%}$ 7.5

30 $\boxed{-}$ 7.5 $\boxed{=}$ 22.50

The tape costs $22.50.

Step 2   Find the price of the tape reduced by $10.

30 $\boxed{-}$ 10 $\boxed{=}$ 20

The tape costs $20.

The better buy is the tape reduced by $10.

Exercise 44-A

Find the final price of each item.

1. 15% discount on a $40 haircut

_____

2. 20% discount on a $345 airline ticket

_____

3. 30% discount on a $69.90 clock radio

_____

4. 25% discount on a $559.50 washing machine

_____

5. 5% discount on a $12,500 car

_____

6. 40% discount on a $429.70 television

_____

7. 10% discount on a $389.59 video recorder

_____

8. 45% discount on a $30.35 concert ticket

_____

Exercise 44-B

CALCULATING

Which is the better buy?

9. A $16.50 compact disc reduced by $2.00 or the same disc reduced 20%?

_____

10. A $140 telephone/answering machine at a 15% discount or a $160 telephone/answering machine at a 25% discount?

_____

11. A $115 raincoat at 30% off or the same raincoat reduced by $40?

_____

APPLICATION

Simple Interest

A bank pays interest to each customer in return for using his money. **Simple interest** is the money paid to each customer on the **principal**, or money deposited into an account.

Example: June deposited $2,500 in her savings account for 2 years. How much simple interest did the money earn at 7%?

To find out, multiply the principal by the interest rate per year and the time expressed in years (y).

Interest (I) = principal (p) x rate (r) x time (t)

I = $2,500   x 0.07   x   2

$$
\begin{array}{ll}
\$2,500 & \longleftarrow \text{principal} \\
\underline{\times \quad 0.07} & \longleftarrow \text{rate} \\
175.00 & \\
\underline{\times \quad \quad 2} & \longleftarrow \text{time} \\
\$350.00 & \longleftarrow \text{simple interest}
\end{array}
$$

The money earned $350.00 in simple interest after 2 years.

Find the interest. Use $I = p$ x r x t.

Principal	Rate	Time	Interest
$ 325	10%	2y	1. _____
$ 500	6%	3y	2. _____
$1,000	7%	$2\frac{1}{2}$ y	3. _____
$1,450	9%	2y	4. _____
$ 800	5%	4y	5. _____

Quiz for UNIT 6

Write the percent.

1. 3 out of 100 _____

2. 16 out of 100 _____

3. 49 out of 100 _____

4. 23 out of 100 _____

5. $\dfrac{13}{100}$ _____

6. $\dfrac{62}{100}$ _____

7. $\dfrac{2}{100}$ _____

8. $\dfrac{1}{25}$ _____

9. $\dfrac{2}{5}$ _____

10. $\dfrac{7}{10}$ _____

Write as a fraction in simplest form.

11. 5% _____

12. 17% _____

13. 35% _____

14. 8% _____

15. 40% _____

16. 29% _____

Write as a decimal.

17. 42% _____

18. 4.7% _____

19. 33.4% _____

20. 3.9% _____

21. 6.3% _____

22. 12% _____

Use a fraction or decimal to find the number.

23. 18% of 40 _____

24. 12% of 52 _____

25. 33% of 60 _____

26. 20% of $149.88 _____

Find the final price of each item.

27. 15% discount on a $50 skirt _____

28. 20% discount on a $68 sweater _____

CUMULATIVE REVIEW

Circle the letter of the correct answer.

Add or subtract. Write the answer in simplest form.

1. $\frac{1}{7} + \frac{3}{7}$

   a. $\frac{4}{14}$ c. $\frac{4}{7}$

   b. $\frac{2}{7}$ d. none of these

2. $2\frac{3}{4} - 1\frac{1}{12}$

   a. $3\frac{1}{3}$ c. $1\frac{8}{12}$

   b. $1\frac{2}{3}$ d. none of these

3. $1\frac{1}{4} + 3\frac{3}{8}$

   a. $4\frac{5}{8}$ c. $2\frac{2}{3}$

   b. $4\frac{4}{8}$ d. none of these

Multiply or divide. Write the answer in simplest form.

4. $\frac{1}{3} \times 7$

   a. $2\frac{1}{3}$ c. $\frac{7}{3}$

   b. $\frac{7}{21}$ d. none of these

5. $8 \div \frac{4}{5}$

   a. 10   c. 8

   b. $\frac{40}{4}$ d. none of these

6. $\frac{1}{5} \div \frac{4}{5}$

   a. $\frac{1}{5}$ c. $\frac{1}{4}$

   b. $\frac{2}{5}$ d. none of these

Write the percent.

7. 37 out of 100

   a. 3.7%   c. 37%

   b. $\frac{37}{100}$ %   d. none of these

8. $\frac{2}{25}$

   a. 2%   c. 8%

   b. 25%   d. none of these

Write as a fraction in simplest form.

9. 3%

   a. $\frac{3}{10}$ c. $\frac{3}{100}$

   b. $\frac{30}{100}$ d. none of these

10. 25%

   a. $\frac{1}{25}$ c. $\frac{25}{100}$

   b. $\frac{1}{4}$ d. none of these

Write as a decimal.

11. 43%

   a. 0.43   c. 0.043

   b. 4.3   d. none of these

12. 23.7%

   a. 0.237   c. 23.7

   b. 2.37   d. none of these

Find the price of each item.

13. 25% discount on a $16.50 movie

   a. $4.00   c. $12.37

   b. $4.13   d. none of these

14. 40% discount on a $210 jacket

   a. $84   c. $250

   b. $126   d. none of these

Book 2

Unit 1
Adding and Subtracting Decimals

Chapter 1 pp. 2–3

Exercise 1-A
1. 1.3 2. 2.9

Exercise 1-B
3. four and one tenth 4. two tenths
5. eighteen and five tenths
6. three and seven tenths

Exercise 1-C
7. 0.8 8. 0.4 9. 0.6 10. 0.1 11. 6.2
12. 9.6 13. 20.5 14. 32.1 15. 50.3
16. 23.6 17. 16.5 18. 43.9

Chapter 2 pp. 4-5

Exercise 2-A
1. 0.09 2. 1.82

Exercise 2-B
3. seven hundredths 4. one and
thirty-four hundredths 5. seven and
nineteen hundredths 6. fifteen and
eighty-six hundredths

Exercise 2-C
7. 0.63 8. 0.02 9. 0.89 10. 0.04
11. 4.16 12. 9.06 13. 15.03
14. 23.34 15. 2.32 16. 6.09
17. 5.12 18. 60.6

Chapter 3 pp. 6-7

Exercise 3-A
1. three thousandths 2. one and one
hundred seven thousandths 3. twelve
and three hundred forty-nine
thousandths

Exercise 3-B
4. 0.324 5. 3.041 6. 5.341 7. 41.008

Exercise 3-C
8. 3 9. 7 10. 1 11. 4

Critical Thinking
12. 6.391; 9.361 13. 6.139; 6.319

Chapter 4 pp. 8-9

Exercise 4-A
1. < 2. < 3. < 4. > 5. > 6. <
7. < 8. = 9. > 10. < 11. > 12. =

Exercise 4-B
13. 0.2; 0.7; 1.7 14. 0.16; 0.27; 0.35
15. 3.3; 3.303; 3.33 16. 4.01; 4.011;
4.10; 4.101 17. 0.32; 0.34; 0.43; 0.52

Mental Math
(See additional answers on page 136.)

Chapter 5 pp. 10-11

Exercise 5-A
1. 3 2. 7 3. 4 4. 7 5. 33 6. 28
7. 39 8. 43 9. 82

Exercise 5-B
10. 3.3 11. 4.7 12. 6.9 13. 9.1
14. 34.1 15. 16.9 16. 43.9 17. 21.1
18. 64.6

Exercise 5-C
19. 3   **20.** 40   **21.** 20   **22.** 9   **23.** 40
24. 40   **25.** 30   **26.** 5   **27.** 20

Exercise 5-D
28. 16   **29.** 3.7   **30.** 16.9   **31.** 113.3
32. 0.80   **33.** 100

Chapter 6 pp. 12-13

Exercise 6-A
1. $13.00   **2.** yes   **3.** $200.00
4. about 10 mi   **5.** $32.00
6. about 280 lb

Chapter 7 pp. 14-16

Exercise 7-A
1. 5.8   **2.** 7.5   **3.** 12.79   **4.** 11.26
5. 16.72   **6.** 21.24   **7.** 85.26   **8.** 61.79
9. 68.6   **10.** 15.60   **11.** 89.20
12. 54.25   **13.** 23.77   **14.** 56.52
15. 22.46   **16.** 29.16   **17.** 103.49
18. 71.69   **19.** 77.31   **20.** 48.52
21. 23.74   **22.** 31.20   **23.** 54.06
24. 57.06

Exercise 7-B
25. 19.5   **26.** 10.62   **27.** 7.59
28. 47.08   **29.** 3.82   **30.** 10.33
31. 14.97   **32.** 36.79   **33.** 18.43
34. 13.85   **35.** 95.96   **36.** 13.77
37. 82.09   **38.** 25.63   **39.** 17.03
40. 67.23   **41.** 36.67   **42.** 50.52
43. 17.38   **44.** 6.52

Exercise 7-C
45. yes   **46.** 10.55

Chapter 8 pp. 17–19

Exercise 8-A
1. 0.6   **2.** 2.2   **3.** 2.9   **4.** 5.1   **5.** 14.0
6. 39.4   **7.** 23.5   **8.** 7.2   **9.** 16.4

10. 35.6   **11.** 38.9   **12.** 54.8   **13.** 1.66
14. 4.85   **15.** 21.41   **16.** 45.44

Exercise 8-B
17. 2.6   **18.** 5.19   **19.** 5.44   **20.** 6.53
21. 4.3   **22.** 3.88   **23.** 0.28   **24.** 0.54
25. 73.25   **26.** 11.19   **27.** 13.98
28. 34.27   **29.** 60.39   **30.** 18.86
31. 81.76   **32.** 51.11

Exercise 8-C
33. $3.11   **34.** $60.07

Calculating
35. 4.8   **36.** 4.9   **37.** $3.11

Application
1. Don Mattingly   **2.** 1985   **3.** .005
4. Wade Boggs

Unit 2
Multiplying and Dividing Decimals

Chapter 9 pp. 24-26

Exercise 9-A
1. 1.44   **2.** 6.66   **3.** 4.92   **4.** 19.0
5. 2,202.6   **6.** 626.01   **7.** 307.2
8. 1,256.13   **9.** 3,767.4   **10.** $3,688.16
11. 3,739.923   **12.** 1,729.266
13. 18,833.74   **14.** $4,662.75
15. 2,371.149   **16.** 1,995.098
17. 1,854.028   **18.** 657.3
19. $7,178.25   **20.** 8,908.90

Exercise 9-B
21. $1,028.25   **22.** $32.85

Chapter 10 pp. 27-28

Exercise 10-A
1. 0.56   **2.** 0.45   **3.** 0.252   **4.** 0.415
5. 11.43   **6.** 0.6798   **7.** 0.78   **8.** 1.1124
9. 49.6281   **10.** 242.08   **11.** 95.0663
12. 103.81   **13.** 374.136   **14.** 64.8646
15. 45.72   **16.** 1.33632   **17.** 22.4568
18. 2,041.02   **19.** 376.473   **20.** 38.52

Exercise 10-B
21. 5,224.511   **22.** 584.12425

Chapter 11 pp. 29-31

Exercise 11-A
1. 11.5   **2.** 1.75   **3.** 1.4   **4.** 21.5
5. 10.4   **6.** 7.42   **7.** 66.1   **8.** 0.018
9. 3.107   **10.** 0.07   **11.** 0.0758
12. 0.258   **13.** 1.04   **14.** 2.4   **15.** 5.47
16. 0.0204   **17.** 0.0547   **18.** 0.028
19. 36.7   **20.** 0.3087

Chapter 12 pp. 32-33

Exercise 12-A
1. 39.7   **2.** 0.9   **3.** 37   **4.** 887   **5.** 463
6. 85.3   **7.** 2,430   **8.** 38,160   **9.** 90

Exercise 12-B
10. 0.87   **11.** 1.283   **12.** 0.004
13. 0.059   **14.** 0.0082   **15.** 0.00893
16. 0.007143   **17.** 0.00416
18. 0.03912

Exercise 12-C
19. 347   **20.** 7.63   **21.** 0.8346
22. 0.016   **23.** 85,100   **24.** 0.09198
25. 0.0659   **26.** 1.207

Chapter 13 pp. 34-35

Exercise 13-A
(See additional answers on page 136.)

5. Wednesday   **6.** conditioner   **7.** 22
8. Friday   **9.** 114

Chapter 14 pp. 36-38

Exercise 14-A
1. 12   **2.** 5.5   **3.** 6.3   **4.** 0.89   **5.** 62.6
6. 0.64   **7.** 31.1   **8.** 12.3   **9.** 65.4
10. 0.36   **11.** 3.21   **12.** 4.25

Exercise 14-B
13. 1.65   **14.** 4.57   **15.** 0.478
16. 0.24   **17.** 0.369   **18.** 0.963
19. 31.4   **20.** 0.85   **21.** 6.3   **22.** 1.25
23. 0.47   **24.** 0.27

Exercise 14-C
25. 2.2

Calculating
26. 3   **27.** 8   **28.** 4

Chapter 15 pp. 39-41

Exercise 15-A
1. 26.3   **2.** 390   **3.** 22.5   **4.** 63.8
5. 45.3   **6.** 230   **7.** 52.3   **8.** 96.4
9. 55.325   **10.** 854.2   **11.** 6.23
12. 62.9   **13.** 3.47   **14.** 1.69

Exercise 15-B
15. 6   **16.** 3   **17.** 15

Application
1. 0.2016   **2.** 0.42   **3.** 28.11   **4.** 0.8649
5. 0.1445   **6.** 27.23

Unit 3
Measurement

Chapter 16 pp. 46–47

Exercise 16-A
1. 120 **2.** 48 **3.** 240 **4.** 720 **5.** 5
6. 3,600 **7.** 360 **8.** 1,440 **9.** 3.5
10. 86,400 **11.** 15 **12.** 1 **13.** 48
14. 40 **15.** 12 **16.** 120 **17.** 2
18. 120 **19.** 30 **20.** 5 **21.** 6
22. 260 **23.** 200 **24.** 8 **25.** 400
26. 12 **27.** 48

Exercise 16-B
28. 21 **29.** 115 **30.** 10,800
31. 2,340

Chapter 17 pp. 48–49

Exercise 17-A
1. 5 hours 19 minutes **2.** 21 minutes
10 seconds **3.** 22 hours 12 minutes
4. 34 minutes 6 seconds

Exercise 17-B
5. 4 hours 25 minutes **6.** 6 minutes
19 seconds **7.** 21 minutes 31 seconds
8. 2 hours 52 minutes

Exercise 17-C
9. 3 hours 15 minutes **10.** 55 minutes

Chapter 18 pp. 50–51

Exercise 18-A
1. 2 hours 15 minutes **2.** 40 minutes
3. 8:25 P.M. **4.** 2:25 P.M.
5. 12:05 A.M. **6.** 5:35 A.M.
7. 5 hours

Chapter 19 pp. 52–54

Exercise 19-A
1. c **2.** c **3.** b **4.** a **5.** b

Exercise 19-B
6. 3 **7.** 20 **8.** 9 **9.** 2 **10.** 100
11. 9 **12.** 2 **13.** 48 **14.** 12 **15.** 7
16. 15 **17.** 5 **18.** 7 **19.** 5,280
20. 5,280 **21.** 28 **22.** 5; 1 **23.** 68
24. 1; 240 **25.** 29 **26.** 92

Chapter 20 pp. 55–57

Exercise 20-A
1. pounds **2.** cup **3.** ounce
4. gallons **5.** gallons

Exercise 20-B
6. 5 **7.** 128 **8.** 4,000 **9.** 12 **10.** 24
11. 16 **12.** 240 **13.** 2.5 **14.** 7
15. 24 **16.** 144 **17.** 2 **18.** 2.5 **19.** 8
20. 3.25 **21.** 74 **22.** 6,062 **23.** 6; 1
24. 17 **25.** 6; 4 **26.** .5

Chapter 21 pp. 58–59

Exercise 21-A
1. −5° F **2.** 70° F **3.** 35° F **4.** 100° F
5. 0° F **6.** −10° F

Exercise 21-B
7. c **8.** a **9.** b **10.** b **11.** b

Application
1. 6:00 P.M. **2.** 4:00 P.M. **3.** 4:00 P.M.
4. 6:00 P.M. **5.** 6:00 P.M. **6.** 7:00 P.M.
7. 7:00 P.M. **8.** 5:00 P.M. **9.** 5:00 P.M.
10. 1:00 A.M. **11.** 2:00 A.M.
12. 2:00 A.M. **13.** 1:00 A.M.
14. 2:00 A.M. **15.** 2:00 A.M.

Unit 4
Adding and Subtracting Fractions

Chapter 22 pp. 64-67

Exercise 22-A
1. $\frac{2}{3}$ 2. $\frac{3}{4}$ 3. $\frac{1}{2}$ 4. $\frac{1}{8}$ 5. $\frac{5}{6}$ 6. $\frac{2}{4}$

Exercise 22-B
7. $\frac{3}{8}$ 8. $\frac{4}{4}$ 9. $\frac{0}{9}$ 10. $\frac{7}{10}$ 11. $\frac{5}{8}$ 12. $\frac{1}{6}$

Exercise 22-C
13. $\frac{2}{3}$ 14. $\frac{1}{5}$ 15. $\frac{7}{8}$ 16. $\frac{1}{2}$ 17. $\frac{3}{4}$
18. $\frac{9}{10}$

Exercise 22-D
19. 4 20. 2 21. 3 22. 4 23. 3
24. 3

Chapter 23 pp. 68-69

Exercise 23-A
1. $\frac{1}{2} = \frac{2}{4}$ 2. $\frac{1}{3} = \frac{3}{9}$ 3. $\frac{3}{8} = \frac{3}{8}$ 4. $\frac{5}{6} = \frac{15}{18}$

5. $\frac{2}{4} = \frac{4}{8}$ 6. $\frac{2}{3} = \frac{6}{9}$ 7. $\frac{1}{4} = \frac{2}{8}$ 8. $\frac{1}{2} = \frac{4}{8}$

9. $\frac{1}{3} = \frac{2}{6}$

Exercise 23-B
10. $\frac{2}{12}$ 11. $\frac{6}{12}$ 12. $\frac{4}{32}$ 13. $\frac{6}{14}$ 14. $\frac{15}{50}$

15. $\frac{2}{14}$ 16. $\frac{4}{18}$ 17. $\frac{15}{18}$ 18. $\frac{24}{28}$

Chapter 24 pp. 70-71

Exercise 24-A
1. 1; 2 2. 1; 3 3. 1; 2

Exercise 24-B
4. $\frac{1}{3}$ 5. $\frac{2}{3}$ 6. $\frac{2}{5}$ 7. $\frac{3}{4}$ 8. $\frac{1}{4}$ 9. $\frac{2}{3}$
10. $\frac{1}{2}$ 11. $\frac{1}{2}$ 12. 1

Exercise 24-C
13. 1 14. 1 15. 4 16. 2 17. 5
18. 1

Chapter 25 pp. 72-73

Exercise 25-A
1. $1\frac{3}{8}$ 2. $2\frac{1}{2}$ 3. 2 4. $1\frac{4}{9}$

Exercise 25-B
5. 4 6. 2 7. 5 8. 5

Exercise 25-C
9. $1\frac{3}{5}$ 10. $2\frac{1}{5}$ 11. $3\frac{1}{3}$ 12. $3\frac{1}{3}$ 13. $2\frac{4}{9}$

14. $1\frac{6}{7}$ 15. $3\frac{1}{2}$ 16. $1\frac{1}{2}$

Exercise 25-D
17. 8 18. $3\frac{2}{3}$

Chapter 26 pp. 74-76

Exercise 26-A
1. $\frac{3}{4}$ 2. $\frac{2}{3}$ 3. $\frac{3}{7}$ 4. $\frac{5}{8}$ 5. $\frac{3}{4}$ 6. $\frac{3}{8}$

7. $\frac{5}{9}$ 8. $\frac{2}{3}$ 9. $\frac{8}{9}$

Exercise 26-B
10. 1 11. $\frac{3}{4}$ 12. $\frac{7}{8}$ 13. $\frac{2}{3}$ 14. $\frac{1}{2}$

15. $\frac{7}{9}$

Exercise 26-C
16. $\frac{3}{8}$ 17. $\frac{4}{5}$ mi

Mental Math
(See additional answers on page 137.)

Chapter 27 pp. 77-79

Exercise 27-A
1. $\frac{1}{5}$ 2. $\frac{2}{3}$ 3. $\frac{1}{4}$ 4. $\frac{1}{2}$ 5. $\frac{2}{3}$ 6. $\frac{1}{4}$
7. $\frac{2}{5}$ 8. $\frac{5}{12}$ 9. $\frac{1}{2}$

Exercise 27-B
10. $\frac{2}{5}$ 11. $\frac{1}{2}$ 12. $\frac{5}{12}$ 13. $\frac{2}{3}$ 14. $\frac{1}{3}$
15. $\frac{3}{8}$

Exercise 27-C
16. $\frac{1}{2}$ mi 17. $\frac{1}{4}$ 18. $\frac{1}{3}$ in.

Chapter 28 pp. 80-81

Exercise 28-A
1. > 2. > 3. <

Exercise 28-B
4. = 5. > 6. > 7. <

Exercise 28-C
8. > 9. < 10. > 11. < 12. < 13. >
14. = 15. >

Estimating
16. 1 17. $\frac{1}{2}$ 18. 0 19. 1 20. $\frac{1}{2}$
21. 1 22. 1 23. $\frac{1}{2}$

Chapter 29 pp. 82-84

Exercise 29-A
1. 2 2. 8 3. 18 4. 4 5. 4 6. 1
7. 12 8. 9

Exercise 29-B
9. $1\frac{1}{8}$ 10. $\frac{1}{2}$ 11. $\frac{3}{4}$ 12. $\frac{3}{4}$ 13. $1\frac{1}{10}$
14. $1\frac{1}{8}$ 15. $1\frac{1}{2}$ 16. $\frac{1}{3}$ 17. $5\frac{5}{6}$
18. $6\frac{13}{14}$ 19. $9\frac{19}{20}$ 20. $3\frac{11}{12}$ 21. $4\frac{11}{24}$
22. $6\frac{7}{15}$ 23. $7\frac{19}{20}$ 24. $12\frac{1}{6}$

Chapter 30 pp. 85-87

Exercise 30-A
1. $\frac{13}{16}$ 2. $\frac{1}{3}$ 3. $\frac{5}{8}$ 4. $\frac{1}{2}$ 5. $\frac{1}{4}$ 6. $\frac{1}{3}$
7. $\frac{1}{8}$ 8. $\frac{3}{10}$ 9. $1\frac{3}{14}$ 10. $2\frac{1}{6}$ 11. $3\frac{1}{6}$
12. $4\frac{4}{9}$ 13. $3\frac{1}{12}$ 14. $2\frac{1}{6}$ 15. $4\frac{1}{2}$
16. $5\frac{17}{24}$

Exercise 30-B
17. $2\frac{1}{4}$ h 18. $\frac{7}{24}$ yd

Chapter 31 pp. 88-89

Exercise 31-A
1. $\frac{3}{8}$ 2. country 3. $\frac{1}{4}$ 4. $\frac{1}{8}$
5. classical 6. The sum of people who like country music and easy listening.

Exercise 31-B
$\frac{1}{8}$; $\frac{1}{4}$; $\frac{1}{8}$; $\frac{1}{2}$

Application
1. $\frac{1}{7}$ 2. $\frac{1}{7}$ 3. $\frac{0}{7}$ 4. $\frac{2}{7}$ 5. 1; 7 6. 2; 7
7. 0; 7

Unit 5
Multiplying and Dividing Fractions

Chapter 32 pp.94-95

Exercise 32-A

1. $\frac{3}{4}$ 2. $3\frac{1}{5}$ 3. $2\frac{1}{3}$ 4. $1\frac{1}{5}$ 5. $8\frac{4}{7}$

6. $10\frac{1}{2}$ 7. $6\frac{2}{3}$ 8. $2\frac{1}{2}$ 9. $3\frac{3}{4}$ 10. $\frac{8}{9}$

11. 1 12. $9\frac{3}{7}$ 13. $2\frac{1}{4}$ 14. $5\frac{1}{2}$ 15. $\frac{6}{11}$

16. $2\frac{7}{10}$

Exercise 32-B

17. 4 18. $1\frac{2}{5}$ mi   19. 16

Chapter 33 pp. 96-97

Exercise 33-A

1. $\frac{1}{6}$ 2. $\frac{1}{20}$ 3. $\frac{1}{42}$ 4. $\frac{5}{24}$ 5. $\frac{3}{14}$ 6. $\frac{7}{12}$

7. $\frac{1}{20}$ 8. $\frac{4}{15}$ 9. $\frac{5}{27}$ 10. $\frac{11}{120}$ 11. $\frac{1}{90}$

12. $\frac{5}{18}$ 13. $\frac{7}{27}$ 14. $\frac{1}{5}$ 15. $\frac{1}{24}$ 16. $\frac{1}{32}$

17. $\frac{7}{25}$ 18. $\frac{6}{25}$

Exercise 33-B

19. $\frac{1}{4}$ c crumbled blue cheese

$\frac{3}{8}$ c yogurt

$\frac{1}{6}$ tsp lemon juice

$\frac{1}{8}$ c sour cream

$\frac{1}{16}$ tsp garlic powder

20. $\frac{1}{6}$

Chapter 34 pp. 98-99

Exercise 34 -A

1. $\frac{5}{6}$ 2. $1\frac{3}{10}$ 3. $\frac{7}{12}$ 4. $\frac{33}{40}$ 5. $3\frac{9}{16}$

6. $11\frac{1}{25}$ 7. 18 8. $15\frac{1}{2}$ 9. $19\frac{1}{2}$

10. $18\frac{1}{5}$ 11. 12 12. 0 13. $6\frac{2}{3}$

14. 16 15. $37\frac{1}{2}$ 16. $3\frac{12}{13}$ 17. $2\frac{7}{9}$

18. $\frac{23}{24}$ 19. $5\frac{2}{3}$ 20. $2\frac{14}{55}$ 21. 11

Exercise 34-B

22. $19\frac{1}{2}$ h   23. $6\frac{1}{2}$ h   24. $\frac{7}{12}$ yd

Chapter 35 pp. 100-101

Exercise 35-A

1. 2 2. 4 3. $\frac{7}{6}$ 4. $\frac{9}{4}$

Exercise 35-B

5. 6 6. 9

Exercise 35-C

7. 5 8. 18 9. 16 10. $26\frac{2}{3}$

11. 16 12. 30 13. 12 14. 25
15. 42 16. 10 17. 10 18. 50

Critical Thinking

19. Greater; you are determining how many times a part is contained in a whole.

Chapter 36 pp. 102-103

Exercise 36-A

1. $\frac{1}{3}$ 2. $\frac{1}{5}$ 3. $\frac{1}{7}$ 4. $\frac{1}{19}$

Exercise 36-B

5. $\frac{1}{9}$ **6.** $\frac{1}{10}$ **7.** $\frac{3}{40}$ **8.** $\frac{2}{15}$ **9.** $\frac{1}{54}$

10. $\frac{3}{14}$ **11.** $\frac{3}{110}$ **12.** $\frac{1}{63}$ **13.** $\frac{1}{16}$ **14.** $\frac{1}{32}$

15. $\frac{1}{14}$ **16.** $\frac{2}{25}$ **17.** $\frac{1}{36}$ **18.** $\frac{1}{6}$ **19.** $\frac{2}{9}$

20. $\frac{1}{12}$ **21.** $\frac{3}{16}$ **22.** $\frac{2}{35}$

Exercise 36-C
(See additional answers on page 137.)

Chapter 37 pp. 104-105

Exercise 37-A

1. $\frac{5}{4}$ **2.** $\frac{4}{3}$ **3.** $\frac{3}{2}$ **4.** $\frac{7}{8}$

Exercise 37-B

5. $1\frac{7}{8}$ **6.** 4 **7.** $\frac{5}{6}$ **8.** $\frac{9}{10}$ **9.** $\frac{1}{2}$ **10.** 8

11. $4\frac{1}{5}$ **12.** $2\frac{1}{2}$ **13.** $\frac{1}{6}$ **14.** $\frac{16}{25}$ **15.** $\frac{3}{4}$

16. 3 **17.** $1\frac{1}{7}$ **18.** $\frac{4}{9}$ **19.** $1\frac{3}{7}$ **20.** 1

21. $\frac{3}{4}$ **22.** 2

Writing in Math
Answers will vary. Possible answer: Dividing by a number gives you the same result as multiplying by its reciprocal. The quotient can be greater because you are determining how many times a part is contained in a whole.

Chapter 38 pp. 106-107

Exercise 38-A

1. $\frac{7}{2}$; $\frac{2}{7}$ **2.** $\frac{24}{5}$; $\frac{5}{24}$ **3.** $\frac{20}{3}$; $\frac{3}{20}$ **4.** $\frac{11}{8}$; $\frac{8}{11}$

5. $\frac{25}{12}$; $\frac{12}{25}$ **6.** $\frac{57}{7}$; $\frac{7}{57}$

Exercise 38-B

7. $\frac{9}{16}$ **8.** $2\frac{2}{11}$ **9.** $2\frac{2}{3}$ **10.** 5 **11.** $3\frac{1}{2}$

12. $\frac{3}{5}$ **13.** $1\frac{1}{4}$ **14.** $\frac{1}{9}$ **15.** $\frac{7}{12}$ **16.** $1\frac{1}{2}$

17. $2\frac{1}{2}$ **18.** $\frac{23}{36}$ **19.** $7\frac{1}{2}$ **20.** $\frac{4}{5}$

21. $\frac{2}{3}$ **22.** $2\frac{2}{3}$ **23.** $2\frac{1}{4}$ **24.** $\frac{7}{15}$

Critical Thinking
25. $\frac{24}{3} \div \frac{6}{8} = 10\frac{2}{3}$ **26.** $\frac{3}{6} \div \frac{24}{8} = \frac{1}{6}$

Chapter 39 pp. 108-109

Exercise 39-A

1. multiply; $9\frac{3}{4}$ **2.** add; $11\frac{1}{2}$

3. divide; $\frac{3}{16}$ **4.** divide; 10

5. subtract; $\frac{5}{12}$ **6.** divide; $\frac{2}{9}$

7. subtract; $7\frac{1}{2}$

Application

1. 1 egg; $1\frac{1}{2}$ tsp baking powder

   1 c bran; $\frac{5}{8}$ tsp baking soda

   1 c flour; $\frac{1}{4}$ c molasses

   $\frac{1}{4}$ c sugar; 1 c buttermilk

   $\frac{1}{4}$ tsp salt; $\frac{1}{4}$ c oil

2. $1\frac{1}{8}$ c flour; $1\frac{1}{2}$ c whole wheat flour

   $\frac{3}{8}$ c sugar; $1\frac{1}{2}$ c blueberries

   $1\frac{1}{8}$ tsp salt; $1\frac{1}{8}$ c buttermilk

   3 eggs; $1\frac{1}{2}$ tsp baking powder

   $\frac{1}{2}$ salad oil; $\frac{3}{8}$ tsp baking soda

Unit 6
Percents

Chapter 40 pp. 114-115

Exercise 40-A
1. 2%   **2.** 69%   **3.** 89%

Exercise 40-B
4. 10%   **5.** 13%   **6.** 7%   **7.** 0%   **8.** 98%
9. 67%   **10.** 25%   **11.** 18%

Exercise 40-C
12. 10   **13.** 25%   **14.** 25%

Chapter 41 pp. 116-117

Exercise 41-A
1. 16%   **2.** 81%   **3.** 1%   **4.** 60%
5. 75%   **6.** 100%   **7.** 50%   **8.** 45%
9. 30%   **10.** 113%   **11.** 40%   **12.** 24%

Exercise 41-B
13. $\frac{3}{100}$ **14.** $\frac{70}{100}$ **15.** $\frac{49}{100}$ **16.** $\frac{10}{100}$

17. $\frac{1}{100}$ **18.** $\frac{6}{100}$ **19.** $\frac{25}{100}$ **20.** $\frac{110}{100}$

21. $\frac{50}{100}$ **22.** $\frac{5}{100}$ **23.** $\frac{9}{100}$ **24.** $\frac{36}{100}$

25. $\frac{45}{100}$ **26.** $\frac{85}{100}$ **27.** $\frac{40}{100}$

Critical Thinking
28. 1   **29.** Change $\frac{6}{25}$ to a percent and compare.

Chapter 42 pp. 118-119

Exercise 42-A
1. 90%   **2.** 17%   **3.** 60%   **4.** 4%
5. 38.7%   **6.** 9%   **7.** 51.7%   **8.** 23%
9. 50%   **10.** 10%   **11.** 49.2%

12. 11.1%   **13.** 70%   **14.** 82.5%
15. 40%

Excersice 42-B
16. 0.37   **17.** 0.98   **18.** 0.03   **19.** 0.429
20. 0.631   **21.** 0.142   **22.** .029
23. 0.85   **24.** 0.09   **25.** 0.043   **26.** 0.24
27. 0.01   **28.** 0.063   **29.** 0.849
30. 0.037

Exercise 42-C
31. .375; 37.5%   **32.** .875; 87.5%
33. .167; 16.7%   **34.** .143; 14.3%

Chapter 43 pp. 120-121

Exercise 43-A
1. $12\frac{2}{5}$ **2.** $15\frac{1}{5}$ **3.** $2\frac{47}{50}$ **4.** $34\frac{2}{5}$ **5.** 28
6. $19\frac{1}{4}$ **7.** $53\frac{9}{10}$ **8.** $54\frac{2}{3}$ **9.** 162   **10.** $136\frac{1}{2}$

Exercise 43-B
11. 19   **12.** 34.78   **13.** 89.9   **14.** 165.6
15. 112.5   **16.** 148.5   **17.** 19   **18.** 75.53
19. 33.6   **20.** 2

Calculating
21. 6.6   **22.** 15.2   **23.** $5.42   **24.** $46.00
25. $96.00   **26.** 13.5

Chapter 44 pp. 122-123

Exercise 44-A
1. $34.00   **2.** $276.00   **3.** $48.93
4. $419.63   **5.** $11,875   **6.** $257.82
7. $350.63   **8.** $16.69

Exercise 44-B
9. the disc reduced by 20%   **10.** the $140.00 machine   **11.** reduced by $40

Application
1. $65.00   **2.** $90.00   **3.** $175.00
4. $261.00   **5.** $160.00

Writing in Math p. 9

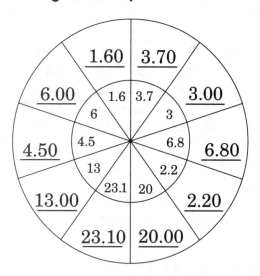

Exercise 13-A p. 35

Sales at **Carole's Comb Out**

	Day	Shampoo	Conditioner	Gel	Mousse	Total
	Monday	3	0	6	0	9
1.	Tuesday	0	18	0	3	21
2.	Wednesday	13	0	0	19	32
3.	Thursday	0	12	16	0	28
4.	Friday	14	10	0	0	24

Mental Math p. 76

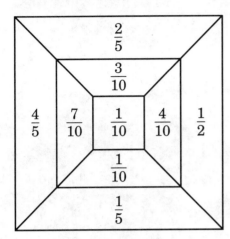

Exercise 36-C p. 103

23.

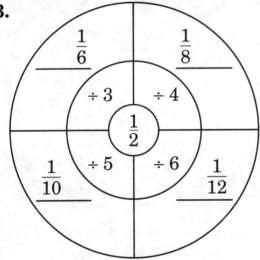

24.

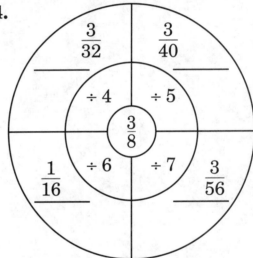

ANSWERS